The Legendary Pine Barrens

Praise for *The Legendary Pine Barrens*

"Gather round this Pine Barrens campfire and listen to Pedersen spin his yarns … a rich brew of the fanciful, the earthy, and the downright creepy."

—Jim Waltzer, author, *Tales of South Jersey*

"The next generation of Pine Barrens legends has arrived, courtesy of Paul Pedersen! His fictional accounts of events set against the mystical backdrop of the pines leave a lasting impression. Readers will love the book's entertaining stories, all told to the beat of a human heart."

—Gabriel Donio, publisher, *The Hammonton Gazette*

"Pedersen is a Pine Barrens treasure. Reading his finely told tales, it's easy to see why the Devil made him do it."

—Dave Hart, co-author, *Mystery of the Jersey Devil* and other stories

"Entertaining and quirky. Pedersen's tall tales are rife with backcountry wisdom and South Jersey flavor!"

—Brenda Kele, assistant to the director,
Noyes Museum of Art, "Hangin'emton"

"Pedersen shines like a gem among the best of the legendary folk tale spinners of South Jersey."

—Linda Stanton, founder, Lines on the Pines

"Paul Pedersen spins tales so clever and engaging you can hardly wait to get to the end to find out what happens. His yarns are sometimes funny, sometimes scary, and sometimes downright spine-chilling. Extraordinary!"

—Barbara Solem, author, *Ghost Towns and Other Quirky Places in the New Jersey Pine Barrens*

The Legendary Pine Barrens

New Tales From Old Haunts

Paul Evans Pedersen Jr.
Illustrations by Jodi Weiss Pedersen

Plexus Publishing, Inc.
Medford, New Jersey

First Printing, 2013

The Legendary Pine Barrens: New Tales From Old Haunts

Published by:
Plexus Publishing Inc.
143 Old Marlton Pike
Medford, NJ 08055

This is a work of fiction. Names, characters, places, and incidents either are the product of the author's imagination or are used fictitiously. Any resemblance to actual persons, living or dead, is entirely coincidental.

"Lure of the Loveladies" and "The Wind Song" first appeared in *Required Restroom Readings*, Mount Misery Publishing, 2009. "The Pine Barrens Blues" (copyright 1987), "Cedar Water Blues" (copyright 1985), and "The Ballad of Raymus O'Dell" (copyright 1990) by Paul Evans Pedersen Jr. © Mount Misery Music.

Library of Congress Cataloging-in-Publication Data

Pedersen, Paul Evans, Jr.
[Short stories. Selections]
The Legendary Pine Barrens : New Tales from Old Haunts / By Paul Evans Pedersen Jr.
pages cm
ISBN 978-0-937548-76-9
I. Title.
PS3616.E295L45 2013
813'.6--dc23

2013003712

Printed and bound in the United States of America.

President and CEO: Thomas H. Hogan, Sr.
Editor-in-Chief and Publisher: John B. Bryans
VP Graphics and Production: M. Heide Dengler

Illustrations by Jodi Weiss Pedersen
Cover art and design by Denise Erickson

www.plexuspublishing.com

To Cookie, who, on May 2, 1987, married—
for better or worse—the *real* Jersey Devil.

And to the Pine Barrens.

Contents

Acknowledgments ix

Foreword xiii

Introduction 1

Welcome to My Pine Barrens 11

The Pine Barrens Blues 13

The Truth About the Jersey Devil 15

Song of the Pine Robbers 27

The Legend of Cassie O'Paier 33

Chakitty-Chikts 43

Strange Towns of the Pine Barrens 49

The Blessed Sands of South Jersey 51

Lure of the Loveladies 55

The Hangin' Tree 61

The Hole in the Pine Barrens 77

Jersey Deviled Clams 83

The Deadbus 87

Jack in the Pulpit 95

The Blood-Stained Waters of the Pine Barrens . . 101

Cedar Water Blues 105

Dr. Mason's Patient 107

The Ballad of Raymus O'Dell 117

The Whiter and Blacker Spikes 119

The Goin's-Ons Out on Purgatory Road 125

Birth of the Tides and Seasons 131

The Legend of Big-Eared Challie 137

The Secret of Salamander Pond 141

Magic of the Silver Queen 157

The Wind Song 171

Goodbye, for Now 179

About the Author 181

Acknowledgments

I started writing *The Legendary Pine Barrens* a long time ago without actually realizing I was doing so, as I drove my kids through the Pine Barrens on the sugar-sand roads that I was pretty sure I could navigate without sinking us up to the doors in sand. They'd ask me questions about tracks they saw, or sounds they heard, or old ruins we'd find, and how I knew where all these places were out in the middle of nowhere. I told them that me and my old junior and senior high school friends would come out here on camping trips and try to get lost. And then I'd just start making up stories that seemed like they might be believable to kids who weren't quite 10 years old yet. So, many thanks and much love to Paul III, Jason, Phil, and Loretta for listening to your "old man" spin his yarns that planted seeds for some of the stories in this book.

Deep appreciation and heartfelt thanks to my wife, Cookie, who has always encouraged my writing, both literary and musical. I appreciate, more than you know, the sacrifices you have made over the years to hold down the fort as I traveled hither and yon in search of "the gold one."

Sincere thanks to my mother, Viola, who always made sure there were lots of books, other than school books, around the house for me to read for fun and entertainment and to dream over. Thanks for your encouragement to pursue a career in writing or music, and for always being there. You're *the best*! And thanks to my late father, Paul Sr., for introducing me to the power of storytelling by scaring me half to death at bedtime. ("I want my liver!")

Thanks to my lovely and talented daughter-in-law, Jodi, for agreeing to do the illustrations for this book. Your talent is amazing, and your illustrations put a wonderful "face" on the stories.

I would like to thank two special teachers in the Collingswood, New Jersey, public school system who made an incredible difference in my life, though I'm sure neither of them know it because I haven't been back there since 1973. The first is Bob Eboch, my eighth-grade science teacher, and the second is Carol Vahlstrom, my 10th-grade creative writing teacher. Mr. Eboch inspired me to want to learn and create, and Mrs. Vahlstrom read Edgar Allan Poe in such a way that not only did you fall head-over-heels for the imagination-evoking power of the words in "The Fall of the House of Usher," but you'd find yourself falling head-over-heels for the soft, hypnotic texture of the voice of the fine lady who was reading it to the class. She made me want to write so I could hear her read my stories. Thank you both for making a difference in so many lives, including mine.

Big thanks to the many, many friends with whom I have performed over the years in the South Jersey music community. Along the way, usually *after* the shows and accompanied by a drink or two, you'd listen to my stories about the Pine Barrens and other delights and encourage me with, "Why don't you write a book?" Well, here it is, just for "youse."

I want to thank some very special "Piney Gals" who have helped and encouraged me not only with writing the book, but for suggesting and supporting the idea of my proposing it to Plexus Publishing, Inc. Thank you R. Marilyn Schmidt, Linda Stanton, and Cathy Antener for your time, encouragement, and continued friendship.

Appreciation is also due to Budd Wilson, preeminent Pine Barrens archaeologist and historian, for pointing out a number of historical inaccuracies in the book. As Budd graciously noted, fiction writers often bend facts in the pursuit of a good story—it's almost a given—yet I took his advice to heart wherever I could, and the book is the better for it. I bear complete responsibility for any remaining errors, omissions, and outright lies.

Thanks to all the professionals at Plexus for welcoming me into the Plexus family, namely Heide Dengler, VP of Graphics and Production; Amy Reeve, Managing Editor; Brandi Scardilli, Editorial Assistant; Kara Jalkowski, Book Designer; Denise Erickson, Cover Designer (amazing cover!); Rob Colding, Book Marketing Coordinator; and Deb Kranz, Sales and Administrative Coordinator. Your support, encouragement, and ideas inspire me, and I am comforted to have such a great team standing with me.

Finally, I extend my deepest thanks and appreciation to my friend John B. Bryans, Editor-in-Chief and Publisher. Your guidance, your ideas, your professionalism, and especially your friendship have become an integral and everyday part of my life. And, you play a hell of a guitar and harp, to boot! Thank you, my friend. Without your helmsmanship this vessel would still be in dry dock, scattered in a whole mess of pieces, and looking for a sail.

Foreword

Welcome to the work of Paul Evans Pedersen Jr.—you are in for a treat. I can't help but smile as I write this foreword to Paul's newest collection of stories, thinking back to the day his manuscript landed on my desk, unsolicited and without fanfare, in an envelope indistinguishable from the dozens of others stacked up all around me.

What I found inside that envelope, however, was anything but typical, as I think you will see soon enough.

Plexus has published some fine novels and short story collections, but until Paul and *The Legendary Pine Barrens* came along, I frankly did not feel we had done justice to southern New Jersey's unique storytelling culture. Legends and lore have been celebrated by "down Jersey" folk for generations. Here, at last, we had encountered a writer who, through the sheer force of his imagination and driven by his passion for the Pine Barrens, could help us extend that tradition into the new millennium.

Make no mistake: These are not your grandfather's stories about the Pines (or, as Paul might put it, they aren't anyone's grandfather's or anyone's grandfather's grandfather's stories about the Pines). Yes, in some cases they bear a resemblance to familiar legends—the Jersey Devil makes several prominent appearances—but they are, indeed, *new* tales. Some self-styled "purists" are sure to take issue with this approach, but I love that Paul has created something fresh and original that is inspired, deeply and genuinely, by the region's rich folklore.

When I met with Paul for the first time to talk about the possibility of publishing his book, I discovered a man who is every bit as impressive as the stories he writes. He's an outstanding singer, songwriter, drummer, and guitarist who has been a chef, fireman, hostler (see "Deadbus" in this collection), newspaper reporter, music producer, moonshiner, truck driver, voice-over actor, antique glass collector, and jewelry-maker—to name just the pieces I've been able to pry out of him. (Humility is one of his traits.) He's a devoted family man with a huge heart and a restless, creative spirit that, from what I've seen, cannot be stanched. I've worked with hundreds of writers in my career, but I can count the truly great storytellers I've known on two hands. Paul ranks among the best.

Mere minutes after that first meeting with Paul, an impressive bit of serendipity presented itself. I popped the music CD he'd given me into my car stereo, and as I pulled out of the restaurant parking lot, the voice that came through the speakers was one I knew instantly. A few weeks earlier on my way to work, I'd been listening to the local college station when a song called "Her Lonely Forgotten" commanded my attention. The recording was stark and powerful, with one of the most mournful and affective country vocals I'd ever heard, and I pulled over to the side of the road to make a note of the artist's name. Now, with this CD playing, I knew in a flash that the musician known as "Paul Evans" and the prospective author named Pedersen were one and the same. It was an amazing moment of realization that, for me, had "kismet" spelled all over it. I've told this story a number of times, and whenever I recommend Paul's album *Agua Noir* to fellow music lovers, I point them to "Her Lonely Forgotten." This song will always give me chills.

The original draft of *The Legendary Pine Barrens* comprised about 100 pages—a little short for a book—so I asked Paul to write five additional stories. He agreed immediately, completed them within a few weeks, and demonstrated one of the most fluid and fertile imaginations I've seen in any writer. There are other things to recommend him. He's a fellow "Fifty-Fiver" (our birth year) and single malt scotch fan, and—along with his wife Cookie—a helluva lot of fun to hang out with. Happily, we have become friends, and he continually inspires me to free my own creative impulses.

Paul was thinking of me and my wife Jenny when he wrote "Magic of the Silver Queen," which appears in this collection. This was among the stories he wrote later, in response to a comment I made about South Jersey's fabulous corn. It's one of my favorite tales of Paul's (I swear I know that witchy woman), and Jenny and I feel honored to be linked with "JayBea" of olde Shamong.

There's a natural flow to the 21 stories and three songs in *The Legendary Pine Barrens*, and reading from beginning to end will assure you don't miss any of the book's hidden gems. That said, some readers are bound to hunt and peck, looking for topics or genres they have an affinity for. Either way, Paul offers something for everyone, from explanations of natural phenomena ("Blessed Sands"; "Hole in the Pine Barrens"; "Blood-Stained Waters"; "Birth of the Tides and Seasons") and new takes on popular legends ("Jersey Devil"; "The Pine Robbers") to mythic and mysterious places ("Strange Towns"; "The Whiter and Blacker Spikes"; "Purgatory Road"), obsessed, avaricious, and intriguing characters ("Cassie O'Paier"; "Lure of the Loveladies"; "Hangin' Tree"; "Big-Eared Challie"), and the otherworldly, frightening, and just plain freaky ("Deadbus"; "Dr. Mason's Patient"; "Salamander Pond"). The tiny, talkative, freedom-loving trolls in "Chakkity-Chikts" make a lasting impression, while "The Wind Song" leaves us on a reflective note, questioning not only the narrator's sanity but our own eyes and ears.

As a closing bit of backstory, while Paul and I were kicking around title ideas, I made the tongue-in-cheek suggestion of *Pine Barrens Legends From a Fevered Brain*. The author tells me he almost choked on his lunch when he read this in email, but I notice he didn't deny its validity!

So, now, sit back, put your feet up if you can, and let Paul Evans Pedersen Jr. transport you back (and forth) in time, between old haunts and places heretofore unexplored. It's a journey of hours that you may hope, as I did, will not too quickly reach the final page.

—John B. Bryans

John B. Bryans has been editor-in-chief and publisher of Plexus Publishing, Inc.'s Book Publishing Division since 1998. He has worked with hundreds of writers and edited and/or published more than 500 original works of fiction and nonfiction since the start of his publishing career in 1979. He waited this long to write his first foreword.

Introduction

One of the things I like best about the Pine Barrens is not only that saying those two words instantly brings to mind a hundred stories you've heard and loved over the years, but that the phrase seems to magically conjure up stories and legends about people, places, and things you haven't heard of yet. Being in the Pines makes you *think*.

The Pine Barrens is not simply a place or a region in southern New Jersey. It's a state of mind, or—more accurately—a state of its own mind that it can share with you, if you're lucky. The Pine Barrens has a feel and a rhythm and a groove all its own. It's secret and ghostly and dark, yes, but in equal measure it is open and expansive, full of life and newness, begging for us to explore it both physically and mentally. Standing in the Pine Barrens, under the right circumstances, *you* could become the object of one of its famous legends.

Or, you could write your own. The thing is, you have to be there.

And that's what happened to me in 1962, when, at the age of 7, I was first introduced to the Pine Barrens. It spoke to me … shared its state of mind with me … and grabbed my heart and mind with a grip as strong as that of the hand of my father, who had pulled me out of the swamp muck I'd sunk up to my chest in at Camp Ockanickon in Medford. It happened during a YMCA "Indian Guides" campout we were on together, and so intense was the suction of the muck that, as Dad pulled me out, my hiking boots were sucked clean off my feet. They are probably still there, in that swamp, to this day.

"That's the Jersey Devil, sport, stealing another pair of boots for his older brother who lives in Smithville," Dad said. "You walked right into his trap. Next time, if ya ain't careful, he gets to keep all of you!" Dad had a way with words, and a way with stories that started rubbing off on me at a very early age.

Reading the story I'd written about that experience to my friends, I could see their eyes and interest widening, word by word, and I became permanently smitten with and under the spell of storytelling and writing. They, too, had heard about this "Jersey Devil" from their fathers and grandfathers, and knew about stories and stuff that lived "down the pines."

And, by the way, that's how south Jerseyans, or "Down Jerseyans" talk: *down*. Destinations are always *down* somewhere. You go down the store for a quart of milk, or down your friend's house to mess around down the cellar. After school, we all went down the lake to catch tadpoles and eels and sunnies, and in the summer we all went down the shore, or down the pool if our town had one. Some of our parents were known to go down the bar, or down the track before it burnt down in 1977. The only time anyone ever went "up," it seemed, was when they were said to be up something called "Schidt's Crick"—in trouble, seemingly, without so much as a paddle. I've always tried to stay away from Schidt's Crick, though I have found myself swimming upstream, against the current, on one of its tributaries a time or two.

Moving on from the YMCA Indian Guides to the Boy Scouts presented me with an even greater opportunity to spend time in the Pine Barrens. People who've never been out there are usually surprised to learn that the areas and regions within the Barrens can be as different as night and day. You can go from the gravelly soil and rolling hills of the northeastern pygmy pine plains to the pin oak and cedar swamps in the southwestern reaches of the Barrens. From bog muck to sugar sand, thick forest to rolling meadow, and rushing rivers and streams to "cricks" and "runs" that barely trickle along, the Pine Barrens has a lot to offer and has always been a wellspring that fills the thirsty, creative sponge of painters, photographers, and writers alike. I began writing more stories along with poetry and quirky little two-line songs about the Pine Barrens to share with my friends.

On a 1966 survival campout with the Boy Scouts one cold, cold night in the southwestern-most reaches of the Pines, I had the occasion to hear what all of us (including the Scout Master) thought and were told was the infamous Jersey Devil. It woke everybody in camp up with a long, blood-curdling scream the likes of which I'd never heard before and have yet to hear again. It certainly was no animal native to New Jersey; it was something un-human. Or *partially* human, leastways. We were told by our Scout Master, who yelled the instructions from *inside* his tent, I might add, to stay awake and alert in our tents until sunrise, at which time we broke camp without having breakfast and went back home to Haddonfield a full day earlier than planned. The Scout Master was badly shook up by whatever had woken us with that hideous scream, and that was the last overnighter he or his son ever took part in.

The incident caused quite a commotion in the church that sponsored our troop. A survival campout being cut a day short on account of "some kind of wild creature at large in the backwoods of Cumberland County" didn't play too well with the church elders or with the family that owned the land on which we'd been camping. The family denied anything remotely similar ever happening in or around their property and dismissed it as "immature camp-fire shenanigans." The church elders admonished our Scout Master, stating that he should have "immediately gathered all present into a prayer meeting and offered hymns up to God-On-High, asking for His divine deliverance for the poor soul who could be so unfortunate as to be out screaming in the woods on such a cold night," instead of "cowering in tents and retreating early the next day." It made a great story, at any rate, and years later I borrowed from the experience when I wrote a song called "The Pine Barrens Blues."

The Barrens with its magic and lure sank its teeth all the way into me, though, during a campout I went on with several friends during Easter vacation in 1969. The four of us were dropped off at Bodine Field by Steve Connors's sister on a Wednesday at about 1 PM. She said she'd be back for us the following Sunday at the same time. Other friends were to join us later in the week. Wayne, Jimmy, Steve, and I set about making camp there, close to the banks of the Wading River. We built half-decent lean-to's, dug a cooking pit, and fashioned something of a root cellar for storing the food we'd brought. We had fires burning all day and night, food to eat, and water to drink from a well down the sand trail; we came to the conclusion, all of us being 14 years old at the time—which is also the youngest recommended age for readers of this book—that this was how we wanted to live for the rest of our lives: off the land and on our own in the Pine Barrens.

On Friday morning we tried to get lost, figuring that by Sunday when Steve's sister came back and couldn't find us, she'd just give up and go home, telling our families that we'd vanished. Try as we might, we couldn't stay lost for more than a few hours at a time. We'd come out to Rt. 563 or Rt. 679, or find the old Evans Bridge Road or the Batona Trail. When we finally tired of trying to get lost, we gave up, went back and re-made our camp, and waited for our incoming friends.

After we ate our evening meal, and seeing nothing of our friends who were supposed to join us, Wayne and I decided it was time to head to the little bar we'd noticed on our way to Bodine Field. It was the closest place around, we thought, that might have a phone we could use to call Timmy and Eddie, our yet-to-arrive friends. We wanted to either make sure they were not coming or find out if they were lost in the woods looking for us. Steve and Jimmy agreed to wait at the campsite in case they showed up and to guard our stuff.

Wayne and I hiked through the woods and found our way to Rt. 563. We started what we knew was going to be a long walk to that little bar at the end of the road. Our conversation got around to the Jersey Devil and the other stuff that was supposed to be going on "out in the Pines" back then, according to the stories we'd heard: weird tribes of albino people that hid in the woods with sticks and clubs, waiting to catch, rob, and bludgeon unsuspecting hikers; Philly and New York mobsters burying their "hits" in shallow graves all over the landscape; real nasty redneck types in old pick-ups without license plates called "Pineys" who would do an Easy Rider number on kids like us from Collingswood just for laughs, and ... there were stories we'd heard about Jersey State Police locking non-locals in their patrol car trunks and bouncing them half to death as they sped along the rutted, bumpy gravel and sand roads out here, then branding their rear-ends with hot, pliers-held paper clips before setting them loose and on their own in the middle of nowhere.

We started walking a little faster and stopped scaring one another with creepy Pine Barrens stories. The sun was nearly down, and there was nothing in sight except the road and the thickest forest we'd ever seen. Hearing a car coming, we instinctively moved away from the road as it approached and then passed us. The brake lights came on as the car slowed and came to a stop, then started to back up toward us.

"What should we do?" I said to Wayne, wondering who was in the car and what their intentions might be. "Just keep walkin'," he said. The car came alongside us, and the driver—a girl of perhaps 18—leaned over and rolled down the passenger-side window.

"You guys need a lift?" she said. "I'm heading into Nesco if you want a ride." She seemed friendly enough and looked mostly normal, so we said, "Sure!" and hopped in.

She said she figured we were campers, as she didn't recognize us, her knowing "all the regular boys in the Pines," and that we were "probably trying to get to the Green Bank." She told us she picked up campers all the time along this road. "It's a *long* walk down to Green Bank from here, ya know," she said. "About five miles."

We hadn't realized it was that far or we'd have never tried it, we told her. At the end of the road, she turned right, and there it was—the Green Bank Inn. As Wayne and I got out and thanked her for the ride, she warned us, "Be careful. Watch what you say to those people in there. See ya."

I've always been tall for my age, and Wayne had a fairly full mustache and beard even at the age of 14, making him look much older than he was. After we walked through the door of the Green Bank Inn, sat at the bar, and looked for a phone, we heard, "What'll you two have?" Wow! We looked at each other, knowing we *had* to go for it. "Two Buds," Wayne said, as calmly as he could, then asked, "Do you have a phone?"

The lady brought two glasses of beer over and pointed toward the back door. "Over there. And don't go out that door! The dog is on the roof and he'll start his damn barkin' again!" We didn't ask her what she meant.

Wayne couldn't get in touch with Timmy and Eddie, but the magic of the Pine Barrens was at work again as he and I sat there and got schnockered on 15-cents-a-glass beer and had a ball talkin' to the old locals at the bar. Just a couple of 14-year-olds from Collingswood and their newfound Piney friends. It was the start of a relationship with me and the Green Bank Inn that continues to this day. We each left with a case of Rolling Rock ponies tucked under our arms, telling each other, over and over again, that we were "going to remember this place."

Years later, I had kids of my own and introduced them to the Pine Barrens when they were very young. I continued to explore and study the many gifts and treasures this remarkable area has to offer, writing songs and stories about what I'd learned and imagined. I've performed countless times at the Green Bank Inn since that first night of finding it at the end of a long road, and even wrote a song about it called "The Screamin' Hollar Inn." The old iron forges and glassworks and paper factories still remain in the form of ruins that dot the Pines in many places. Each of these ghost towns has a history and stories of its own, and with a little research and some imagination, I have come to regard the Pine Barrens as not only a legendary place, but as home. It is where my heart is.

One of the "new legends" I remember starting with my kids began one afternoon while we were exploring the Washington Turnpike-Bulltown Road area that lies behind Batsto in Burlington County. Coming upon some deep horse tracks, my son Paul blurted out, "They must have been made by the Jersey Devil, Dad!" "Indeed they were," I said, and then, seeing that the kids were growing nervous and a little frightened, I instructed my son Jason to go to the car and retrieve a Mason jar I'd bought at a yard sale from the back seat. We all bent down around the tracks and I opened the jar, then had them carefully scoop all of one of the tracks into the jar. After screwing the lid back on, I said, "Now, as long as that track stays sealed in this Mason jar, the Jersey Devil will never come after you."

That sealed jar full of sand stayed in my daughter Loretta's bedroom closet until she grew up and left the house many years later. It's still around here somewhere and was the "seed" to one of the stories you'll find in this collection, "The Blessed Sands of South Jersey."

These days, I'm thrilled to see my kids passing on the Pine Barrens traditions, legends, and stories to *their* children. The wife and I took a carload of grandkids (we have 10) to the infamous town of Leeds Point awhile back and showed them the birthplace of New Jersey's most famous son. There were a lot of wide, wary eyes as they stood there at dusk on a summer's evening, looking around—and darned if we didn't see what looked like the ol' Devil himself climbing down the outside of a chimney of a house there in the woods. We have the pictures to prove it!

I know that trip will stay with my grandkids for the rest of their lives, and, maybe ... who knows, but just maybe, it will be the seed that starts a new legend or song by another author in the family on his or her own writing journey. And I hope this collection of stories will stay with *you*, and that you'll share them, and perhaps they'll plant some seeds in the imaginations of you and yours for years to come. The Pine Barrens are, after all, legendary for spawning new ideas and stories, and filling lots of empty canvasses with rainbows of color.

Welcome to My Pine Barrens

So, you'd like to hear some stories about the Pine Barrens? Seems like *lots* of folks want to hear stories about my Pine Barrens these days. Why not? This is a magical, mysterious place, indeed!

First of all, the Pine Barrens is a huge area of ancient forests, wetlands, bogs, and swamps in southern New Jersey. It has remained unchanged for a long, long time, although a lot of stupid people keep trying to change that: builders and land developers and the rest of that greedy bunch. But the Barrens has its own way of dealing with them, so not to worry too much.

There are a lot of special things, in and about the Pine Barrens, that happen here and nowhere else on Earth. Why, there are 30-some plants growing here that you couldn't find anywhere else in the world. Certain frogs and salamanders, snakes, birds, and other creatures live here, and call *only* the Pine Barrens of South Jersey home. On top of that, the largest reserve of pure water on the East Coast lies under the Pine Barrens.

What's more, the Pine Barrens is the only place "he" calls home. C'mon, now—you know who I mean! The famous 13th son of old Mrs. Leeds … the *Jersey Devil.* He's still here, to this very day. Lurkin' about in the misty, quiet dead of the night, sneakin' hither and yon, and waitin' to scare the sweat out of anyone who happens to make his acquaintance.

So many other legends and stories are alive here, too. Where they've always been. Where they belong. And where they'll always stay. Like the legend of Joe Mulliner and his gang of Pine Robbers. Then there's the legend of Pastor Jack Morrison, and how he tried to bring the old hermit in the woods to the Lord and disappeared in a cranberry bog for his troubles. And it was here in the Barrens that an old Indian Chief cursed the rivers and streams to be forever stained red with the blood of his tribe. Then, too, there's the story of the Chakitty-Chikts—thousands of tiny trolls that *still* live in the Pines.

So what makes the Pine Barrens so special, you ask? Well, sit back and relax awhile, and I'll tell ya some stories, my friend. Stories from the south of Jersey.

Stories from the Pine Barrens.

The Pine Barrens Blues

In the backwater marshes,
Where the cranberries grow.
The water takes on the color
Of wine as it flows.
And every evening the sun's fire
Drowns in the bays,
And all the creatures that live here,
They have their own special way.
They're true,
These Pine Barrens Blues.

The folks that live in the Barrens,
Have a story they tell.
They say the old Leeds woman,
She bore a child from Hell.
After his birth, he took wings on,
And flew out into the night.
They say you'll still hear him screamin'
When the conditions are right.
They're true,
These Pine Barrens Blues.

Out where the scrub oaks are growin'
And where the years forget time,
All the life that can happen
Still happens deep in the Pines.
You'll see the Jack-in-the-Pulpit, and a devil or two,
And when the moonlight shines full, here,
You'll see some other things, too.
They're true.
These Pine Barrens Blues.
Yes, they're true.
These Pine Barrens Blues.

The Truth About the Jersey Devil

So, my friend, you think you've heard all the versions of all the stories and know all of the twists, turns, nooks, and crannies there are concerning the Pine Barrens's most notable resident, the Jersey Devil? Well, there's one more that you need to learn about. The *real* one. The *true* one. The one that all the others have borrowed this, that, and the other from. The only one that *could* be true, when push comes to shove. And this is it.

They say that in the far eastern edge of Atlantic County, between present-day Conovertown and Leeds Point, there is a particular road of sugar sand that, at first, seems like all the rest of the sugar-sand roads that traverse the Pine Barrens. It winds and weaves and rises and dips, and is shaded by pine, oak, and sumac vines, and tall old red and eastern white cedar. The road goes real grabby here and there, as the locals say, and is quite capable of swallowing a car up to its windows, and then some, in its pure-white, sugary-soft silica sand.

As the road heads dead-straight east in a long and barely noticeable decline, the ever-thickening vines and stands of ancient cedar gradually block out most all of the sunlight, even at high noon. The ground becomes a wet, black, gooey swamp on each side of the road, and a strange, eerie feeling of danger and foreboding seems to wrap itself around everything and anyone in sight.

Strange, acrid smells begin to stir in the air. The earthy, rotting thickness of the swamp and the light, aerosol-ish perfume of the several species of pine, along with that of various other indigenous trees, mosses, ferns, and orchids, combine into an unusually wild yet uniquely attractive broth of olfactory porridge that covers everything like a heavy wet cloak.

After a quick bend to the right, all at once the road stops dead in its tracks, changing immediately into the open vastness of the back-bay marshes, wetlands, and grasslands. Sugar-sand and gravel roads are replaced by ribbons of tidal waters that snake and sneak through the tall elephant and salt grass; if followed long enough, these streams will lead the bold traveler into the open bay and, soon after, into the mighty North Atlantic.

It is said, however, that if you turn to your left about 100 feet before the road dead-ends, and then carefully venture into the dark thickness of swamp and cedar and hanging vines, you will come to the best-kept secret in the Pine Barrens—a place that only very, very few know about. This is the Mating Pool, and it is here that, revealed now for the first time in print, the Jersey Devil was born!

It all started in the summer of 1698, when the infamous pirate Captain William Kidd of Dundee, Scotland ("Cap'n Kidd," as he's known in modern times) and a few of his men came ashore in a small boat near what is now Leeds Point, leaving their main "pirate ship" anchored and guarded safely off shore in the mouth of the bay. They were off-loading a shipmate, one Timmy Jones, who had become crazy and violent toward Kidd and the other men aboard ship while at sea.

Some said Jones went mad after drinking whiskey that had been contaminated with seawater during the long voyage. Others said it was either pieces of rancid pork or the uncooked legs from seabirds he'd captured, hidden in his bunk, and gnawed on at night for a snack that sent him mad. It could have been, and no doubt was, a combination of all of it. No matter. He was now insane and entirely mute, able only to grunt, and Cap'n Kidd wanted him off the boat.

Kidd chose not to kill or abandon Jones at sea, as they'd been lifelong friends, so he opted to tie him up, take him to shore, and leave his fate to the wild woods where he'd at least have some chance at survival. "He will not die directly by my hand or sword," Kidd vowed to the ship's company.

So, Kidd and Jones, along with three other men brought along to guard Jones, rowed the small boat slowly and carefully through and along the tidal rivulets of the grasslands, and finally went ashore on the mainland.

After they beached and secured the boat, they walked about 30 yards into the forest, where they found what looked like a large, uncovered well in a small clearing. The well was about 3 feet across and was surrounded by a wall of Jersey bog stone that wasn't more than 2 feet high all around it.

"This is as good a place as any," said Kidd to the men who were guarding Jones. "Lash him to that tree limb there, near the well, and we'll be off."

As the men tied the rope that was already binding Jones to a tree limb about 10 feet from the well, Kidd said to him, "Timmy, me boy, you've lost yer mind, lad, and I can stand thy shenanigans and thy tirades on me ship no longer. May God, or whoever be with ya, tend to ye now, lad, as I can do it no more." Jones bared his teeth and grunted his displeasure, flailing and kicking at his bindings, but to no avail. The ropes held tight.

And with that, Kidd and the other men left Jones lashed to a cedar in the wild swamplands of what would later be known as eastern Atlantic County, New Jersey, at the mercy of whatever the gods of fate and darkness might bring him.

What they brought him was Amanda Leeds.

Amanda, a 40-year-old widow woman who lived alone in a cabin not far from the clearing, had been hiding in the woods, watching as the pirates came ashore, leading the tied-up man into the forest. She watched secretly as they lashed him to the tree, spoke their goodbyes to him, and left him alone in the wild woods of the swamps. Amanda wondered why they would do this to one of their own men, but not for very long.

You see, she was probably as crazy as Jones. Perhaps even crazier, and for a lot of reasons.

Slowly and cautiously, as soon as she was sure the other men were gone for good, Amanda made her way to the little clearing by the well. She stood there in front of Jones, staring at him, waving and smiling at him every now and again, without saying a word. Each time she smiled, Jones would grunt back at her. And each time he grunted, Amanda would smack herself in the forehead with the palm of her hand and roll her eyes. This would cause Jones to laugh wildly, which caused Amanda to laugh wildly, and before long, the two of them were laughing wildly for no reason at all, there, in the middle of the godforsaken swamps of the Pine Barrens.

After some time had passed and they'd grown tired of their little act and stopped laughing, little by little Amanda began to move closer and closer to Jones, who watched her intently. He liked the way her long dress moved easily in the breeze, seeming to dance and sway along with her long, strawberry-colored hair. He became instantly smitten by her, amazed at the intensity of her ice-cold blue eyes. It had been a long time since he'd been this close to an attractive woman.

Just a few feet from him now, Amanda said, almost in a whisper, "Don't you just love how the forest looks, sounds, and smells just now? My face strangely feels like I've been in the sun too long, and yet I haven't been. Do you ever feel like that?"

Jones grunted, and the look on his face convinced Amanda that he knew, indeed, how she felt. She became more at ease with him, though he was still bound to the tree, and she started feeling almost like she could trust him not to harm her.

She smiled and continued. "You know, some of the very oldest of the Lenni-Lenape tribe tell of a tribal memory that they keep very secret about this place. It's about that well there, especially. They say that at exactly the right time on exactly the right summer's night, during exactly the right year that only comes along so often, when the water is exactly between the right saltiness and sweetness in the well, this place somehow calls to all the creatures that live here and brings them together. Some of them stand or sit or lay on that wall, and still others get *into* the well, and they all spend the night together, copying each other's voices and calls whilst coupled with their mates, until the morning comes. They call it the Night of the Kamonaweehawwana Year."

It was growing darker and darker, and they looked at one other for a long time after Amanda had finished her story. There was a strange passion growing between them, slowly at first, and then it suddenly seemed to rise and swell from inside both of them, to the point that they could almost see and touch and smell it. Amanda said, "If I untie you, will you be a gentleman and not harm me?"

Jones grunted and nodded his head, and Amanda saw in his eyes that he was telling her the truth. She went about untying him, throwing the rope into the woods. At last, Jones stood there, rubbing his chest, arms, and hands together, getting his circulation moving again, and grunting his pleasure and thanks to Amanda for freeing him. He outstretched his hands toward her, let out one big, loud grunt, and smiled.

"Oh! You're welcome!" Amanda said. And with that, she held out her arms, and the two kissed and embraced for a long time, moving slowly but ever closer to the well.

Amanda was now sitting on the wall of the well with her arms around Timmy Jones's chest. As they were embracing and sharing another long kiss, she wrapped her legs around him so he couldn't move, then leaned back and pulled him with her down into the well.

They spent the entire night coupled together in the warm water in the well, holding each other close, kissing and laughing, looking up at and listening to and mimicking the calls and songs of all the other mating creatures that had gathered on the wall above them.

They could see the silhouettes of wolves, foxes, bats, wild horses, raccoons, and other wild animals of the swamps and woods in the moonlight, staring down at them. It went on and on and on.

A warm, gentle rain came in the morning and washed away the fur and feathers and other things that were left on the wall during the previous night by the participating creatures. Amanda and her man, sometime just before dawn, slipped into the nether world, exhausted and unable to free themselves from their watery bliss. They died peacefully together, entwined forever as happy lovers, never to be seen or heard from again.

Well … kinda.

As the summer continued, the water in the well kept its special, saline-like sweetness. It remained quite warm, at just under 98 degrees, well into November. That, together with the furs, feathers, juices, and microbes that were washed into the well during the morning rain, along with the fertile remains of Amanda Leeds and Timmy Jones, produced a mass of the strangest goo imaginable down in the dark well.

What's more, it was alive.

It clung to the side of the well, feeding and growing off the microbes and algae that thrived in the water, along with the small insects, rodents, and other animals that happened to fall down into the well throughout that summer and fall.

The elders of the Lenni-Lenape tribe in the area sensed that this was going to be a so-called Kamonaweehawwana Year, and so they gathered in the clearing near the well at the end of November and waited for that special night. For several days and nights they danced, ate, and chanted up at the gods.

Then, one night, just before December, it happened. There came from the well a sound like a child crying. Minutes later, it sounded like growling. Suddenly, up from the well, and seemingly from the very bowels of the earth, came a horrific scream, along with the sounds of wild flutterings and scrapings, splashings, and thumpings. The entire tribe stood there, chanting, "She-HOOO! She-HOOO! She-HOOO!" with their arms raised straight up in the air and the sparks from their fire flying all about.

Up from the well flew a creature that had huge, bat-like wings, a serpentine tail, hindquarters like a wolf, sharp-clawed hands like a raccoon, a head and hooves like a horse or mule, a deer's antlers, the cunning eyes of a fox, and the shrill, hissing call of a marauding screech owl. In spite of these animal characteristics, it seemed almost human as it perched on the wall of the well, looking at, and seeming to reason with, watch, and consider the tribesfolk.

Indeed, this creature was the homogenized, living, breathing conglomerate of all of the creatures that had met and mated at the well that night in early summer.

Indeed, the Lenni-Lenape had witnessed the birth of the very Jersey Devil himself.

As the tribe continued to yell "She-HOOO!" at the creature in unison, it finally flew away into the swamp. And there, in a South Jersey swamp in late November, came what would later be known as the first Thanksgiving, as this "She-HOOO!"-ing ritual was later taught to and celebrated with the arriving Englishmen, in the belief that its annual celebration would ward off any unwanted visits by the creature. People have been "shooing" the Jersey Devil ever since.

It's no wonder that the Jersey Devil was never reported to have bothered the Indians. They were the first people he saw after being "born" from the well, so it's just good logic that he figured they were his parents.

Over the years, folks have wondered who "Mother Leeds" *really* was, and many have expressed great skepticism as to how a new-born child could possibly and almost instantaneously morph into a winged, hoofed creature and fly up a chimney. Perhaps the old stories and legends were wrong all along, and were told to hide the truth, as reported here. Perhaps it wasn't a chimney at all, but an enchanted well, deep in a Pine Barrens bog that the creature flew up and out of.

This well, for a time, became known as "the sex pool" by the locals in the area, most of whom spoke with a lisp due to the rampant tooth decay prevalent in the area. As a result, it sounded like they were saying "cess pool." Down Jersey folk have been referring to anything resembling a brick-lined well or small pool in their backyard as a "cesspool" ever since.

Folks have wondered, too, how the Jersey Devil keeps showing up, generation after generation, for some 300 years now, but he never seems to age from the first accounts of his appearance. Perhaps the continued and returning Kamonaweehawwana Years, along with the undeniable power of the age-old call of nature that's been heard by generations of skinny-dipping lovers on warm summer nights since the dawn of time will continue to produce new Jersey Devils. Forever.

After all these years, some things haven't changed in and around the Pine Barrens of South Jersey. The first is that it's a wise man (or woman) who knows when a Kamonaweehawwana Year is at hand, so that he or she can prepare for the next outbreak of Jersey Devil sightings. Secondly, parents *still* yell out at their children playing in South Jersey backyards, "Hey, you kids! Stay away from that damn cesspool!"

Song of the Pine Robbers

If you ever find yourself wandering along the sandy roads of the Pine Barrens at sundown in June somewhere near Washington Tavern, you just might hear someone, suddenly, unseen in the dense forest, playing a little ditty, over and over again, on a flute. And just as suddenly, you might hear the strange, ghostly sound of whip-poorwills calling to each other. There's a reason for that, friend. You see, it's the Pine Barrens's long-ago memory of a wicked man and his gang, a lonesome song, and a lost kiss.

A long, long time ago, way back in the 1700s, there was a gang of men known as the Pine Robbers who used to roam around in the Pine Barrens. The leader of this gang was a man by the name of Joe Mulliner. Joe and his gang, who were Tories—colonists who sided with the King of England before America won its independence—were known to steal silver and gold from the folks who lived in the Pine Barrens. They'd either spend it on wild whiskey-drinking parties or bury it and come back for it later, when they needed it for supplies and the like.

Now, even though Joe was a wicked man, he had one soft spot in his heart, and that was for music. Joe loved to play the flute. On more than one occasion, he and his gang would go into a tavern at night, where people were drinking and dining, and the gang would hold the patrons at gunpoint, forcing them to listen while Joe played his flute. And it was always the same, unmistakable little tune people had to listen to, as Joe only knew how to play one song. He called it "The Pine Robbers Song." And, legend says, it was taught to Joe by the Devil, in return for his successful life of crime and his soul when he died. While Joe played his song, the gang would rob everyone in the tavern. Then they'd leave, laughing, and ride off into the dark Pine Barrens night, the sound of Joe's flute disappearing with them.

During one such hold-up, in June 1781 at Washington Tavern, near the crossroads of Washington and Godfrey Bridge roads, Joe again played his song on the flute while his gang held up all the patrons. As the thieves were leaving the tavern, a beautiful girl came out and told Joe that she simply loved the little song he had played, even though she was quite upset that he had just robbed her parents.

Well, Joe was instantly smitten with this young beauty. He asked her, over and over again, if she really liked the music he'd played. She told him, over and over again, that, yes, she did indeed.

Joe approached her, took her hand, bowed his head, and handed her five gold coins that had been taken during the robbery. She thanked him and gave her name as Martha. She explained that she and her parents ran the iron furnace nearby and that the work was hard and didn't pay much, and that she was truly thankful that Joe had returned the gold he'd taken from them.

They stood and looked at each other for several moments, and then Joe bent down and tried to kiss her. Martha pulled away and told Joe that she would only kiss him if he came to her home on the following Saturday night and played the flute for her on her front

porch. Joe smiled at her and told her that, sure enough, he'd be there on Saturday with his flute and expecting his kiss.

As Joe and his gang rode away into the night, his gang warned him that meeting the girl on Saturday was a bad idea. Martha's home was several miles from their hideout in the Pines and out in the open on Pleasant Mills Road. Not to worry, Joe said—he had a plan. The gang would hide in the bushes and trees around the girl's house, and warn him if anyone was coming.

The following Saturday night, just as it started getting dark, Joe's gang hid in the bushes and trees around Martha's house. Joe walked up the steps and started playing his flute on Martha's front porch. Finally, she came to the door and walked out on the porch with Joe. She looked like she'd been crying, but she managed to smile. All the members of Joe's gang saw Martha come out, dressed in a beautiful white gown. The gang started whistling, a little three-note whistle, like when men whistle at pretty girls.

Just as Joe was bending to kiss Martha, about 30 sheriff's deputies came running from inside the house. Joe, so shocked that he couldn't move, was captured that night on the porch. Many of his gang members were captured, too, as they tried to run.

The Pine Robbers, finally, were no more.

Well, they say they hanged Joe Mulliner and many of the Pine Robbers in Burlington soon after for the horrible crimes they had committed over the years. However, as it was the custom back then to put a black hood over a man's head before hanging, none of the witnesses could ever feel *really* sure it *was* Joe who was hanged on the end of that rope. There are those who say that Joe escaped the hanging and made his way back into the Pine Barrens, where he still plays his Pine Robbers song in and around Washington Tavern and Martha's Furnace … waiting for Martha and his lost kiss … and where the ghosts of his gang, who've come back in the form of the whippoorwills, still whistle their strange catcalls from the bushes and trees as the sun sets in the Pine Barrens.

But be forewarned, friend. If you ever hear the "Pine Robbers Song," enjoy the moment for what it is, then forget it! For many a good man who has heard that song, and tried to learn it, add something to it, and then play it to an audience for silver and gold, has lost his soul … and spent the rest of eternity searching for a lost kiss.

The Legend of Cassie O'Paier

It's a well-established fact that the very ground folks walk on, and, in all honesty, take for granted in the Pine Barrens, is magical.

After all, where else do those famous Jersey tomatoes, the best-tasting tomatoes in the world, grow and come from? Where else does the "magical, secret mud" that's used to rub each and every baseball that's thrown in a Major League Baseball game come from? Where else is the sand so pure that it needn't be washed before being blown into some of the world's most prized and collectable glass bottles and art objects? Where else can you find earth whose seemingly magical filtration properties have created a subterranean ocean holding 17 trillion gallons of the purest water in the world?

Magical, indeed, is this ground we walk on.

But did you know that a teapot's-worth of Pine Barrens sand and the lusty conjurin's of an old Mount Misery "doctor" are responsible for a constellation that's still seen in the Pine Barrens night sky? Why, of course it is!

And here's how it came to pass.

They called him Ishka Baha, and he'd lived in Mount Misery for as long as anyone out that way could remember. Originally from Scotland, folks said, he was old, grumpy, bearded, and white-haired, and he didn't have two nice words to say to anyone, even when they came to him for help. And that was often, you see, because Ishka Baha was known in and throughout the early 1700s as "Dr. Ishka," or "Dr. Baha," or "Dr. Ishka Baha" by everyone in that part of the Barrens.

He wasn't *really* a doctor. He never went to a school of any kind and couldn't write his own name. But he had the ways and the "form-la's" of the "medicinals," as folks were fond of calling them, claiming they were better than the herbs and barks and berries and owl toenails and pickerel beaks and a thousand other things that grew, flew, swam, and hopped in the Pine Barrens that were used to cure their ills before Ishka came along.

Dr. Ishka claimed he could cure everything from whooping cough to glass burn to "innin's rot" and "seat bite" ("innin's rot" being cancer and "seat bite" being hemorrhoids). Nary a day went by that Dr. Ishka wasn't workin' on a tea or making a poultice for someone suffering from one malady or another out in the Barrens. Folks would pay him for his services if they had the money or promise to pay him when they got it. In the Pine Barrens, it was usually the latter. This led to the once-popular Piney saying that "Nobody wants to pay for yesterday's Ishka Baha."

Back in July 1708, a young couple, newly married, came to Dr. Ishka's cabin out in the woods one day around noon. Sean and Cassie O'Paier were their names, and they'd come to see if Dr. Ishka would recommend a healthy diet and perhaps mix up some supplemental herbs, vitamins, and teas, as the couple was planning to start a family, and they wanted Cassie to be in peak prenatal health. For Cassie, it seemed that regardless of how much she ate, she stayed at the same weight. The O'Paiers wanted the good doctor to help plump Cassie up before she got with child and had come to seek his counsel and services.

No sooner had he laid eyes on her than Dr. Ishka Baha fell head over heels in love with Cassie. Married or not, it didn't matter. He'd never seen anyone or anything so beautiful, and he felt his very spirit being drawn into her like breath itself. He nearly began to shake, so completely infatuated was Ishka Baha.

Composing himself during that first meeting, the doctor told Cassie she was to come to his cabin each day in order to partake of a special vitamin and herb concoction he would brew for her. The tea had to be drunk while it was very fresh, immediately from the steep, he explained, and special equipment would be used to make it. Thus, she *had* to come to his cabin to be treated, he said. There certainly was no sense in Sean coming to the appointments, he added; the treatments were going to be expensive, and Sean would need to double his work efforts in order to pay for them.

So, every day for 6 months, Cassie trekked through the woods to Dr. Ishka's cabin, where, immediately upon her arrival, the doctor would have her sit in his special doctorin' chair as he treated her with a freshly made cup of tea that she exclaimed on many occasions tasted like "old, soapy rainwater." He would sit there the whole time, beside and slightly behind her on his little wooden stool, and just stare and stare and stare at her, saying softly, "Just keep sipping, my dear, just keep sipping …"

Six months passed, yet Cassie *still* showed no weight gain. In fact, she lost weight and had begun to shake at times, with the sensation of spiders crawling on her arms. One night, as they were having dinner, Sean broke down and told Cassie he was nearly worked to the bone trying to earn enough money to continue her treatments, but the work was drying up, and, since there was no improvement anyway, she should consider quitting those "damned tea parties." Cassie angrily yelled back at Sean that it was no "tea party," that she hated the tea and she doubly hated the way the doctor stared and stared at her as she sat in that uncomfortable "doctorin' chair" he made her sit in for hours every day.

That settled it. The O'Paiers agreed that the visits to Ishka Baha were over.

The next day, Cassie walked through the woods to Dr. Ishka's cabin. He was waiting for her at the front door, holding it partially open as usual. Cassie stopped short of going all the way across the porch to the front door, and said, "I cannot continue the treatments, doctor, as there is no money left and the treatments don't seem to be working anyway. In fact, I seem to be getting thinner."

The doctor stood there, dumbstruck and frozen, and couldn't speak for a moment. He just stared at Cassie and seemed about to cry. Suddenly, he smiled, bowed his head a little bit, and said, "Ah, Miss Cassie-O, I understand the troubles you're havin'. Let me at least give you something, free of charge, that you can use at your home. It may just help you along the path I'm tryin' to lead ya down."

Cassie thought about the doctor's offer for a moment and didn't see that any harm could come from accepting a gift. "All right," she said, "but then I really must be getting home."

Dr. Ishka disappeared into his cabin for a short time and then came back with a silver teapot that he handed to Cassie. She looked at it as she held it in her hands, amazed at its striking beauty. It almost frightened her, it was so beautiful.

"Oh, Doctor," she protested, "I cannot accept such a beautiful item as this!"

"Of course you can, and you *must*!" the doctor said forcefully, startling her. "It will help you, so long as you follow the simple directions inscribed there—on the spout."

Cassie looked closely at the teapot's spout, and there, meticulously carved in the silver, were the words, "Water Me."

She looked at the doctor in confusion. "*Water me*?"

"Yes, Cassie," he said gently. "Simply open the top each and every morning, and pour a cup of water into the pot. Leave it by itself on a table or shelf and continue to water it. You'll see why before too long."

Cassie thanked the doctor again and again for the teapot, and then started home. As she walked along through the Pine Barrens, she opened the top of the pot. It seemed to be filled with pure, white sand. She wet her finger with her tongue, poked it in the pot, and tasted it. There was no taste. It *was* sand. She picked up a twig from the ground and stirred the sand around, looking for seeds, roots, or anything that might need watering, but there was nothing in that pot except perfectly pure white sand.

At dinner that night, she told Sean what had happened that day at the cabin, how the doctor seemed ready to cry when she told him she had to quit the treatments, and about his teapot gift and the odd instructions carved into the spout. Sean said, as he ate the clam stew Cassie had prepared, that he thought Ishka Baha was a quack who wanted only to stare at his wife sitting in that chair. He planned to write to the governor of the colony and to the King himself, and demand that they not only look into the doctor's practicing procedures but force him to return the monies they'd paid for the worthless and questionable services rendered. Someone like that, Sean said, could be the ruination of the civilized world if he was allowed to continue in his practice, such as it was.

Day after day, Cassie would have her morning coffee at her kitchen table, where, right in the middle, sat the teapot Dr. Ishka had given her. Each morning, she opened the top and poured in a cupful of water. Weeks that turned into months went by, but nothing ever grew or even sprouted from the teapot.

What *was* happening, however, was that Cassie was getting thinner still and had begun to lose her hair. Not long after her hair fell out, she started losing the use of her legs, and then her arms. She was soon completely bedridden, and within a few days, she was at death's door.

Just before Cassie passed away, she whispered to Sean, who had stayed faithfully by her bedside throughout her ordeal, "Dear, don't forget to water the teapot Ishka Baha gave me when I'm gone."

Those were her last words.

As Sean watched Cassie slip away, he was devastated with grief. Suddenly, the grief turned into anger. He ran from her side and into the kitchen, and picked up the teapot—the teapot he was now blaming for his wife's death … the teapot given to her by someone who,

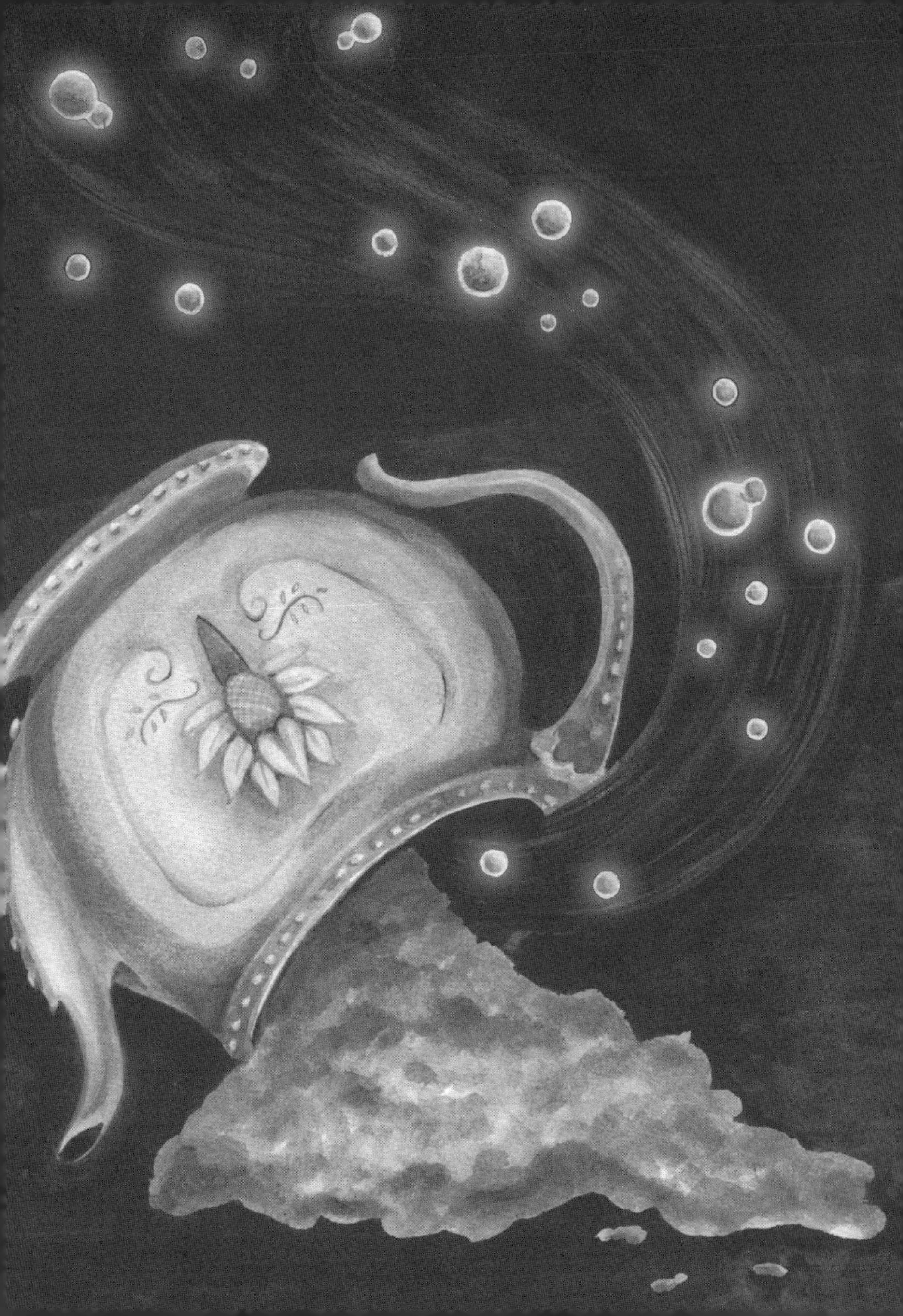

little by little, had robbed them nearly blind as he sat and gawked at his wife, making her condition worse, and finally killing her. The teapot given to her by one Ishka Baha!

With all his might, Sean threw the teapot out the front door, screaming, "Damn you, Ishka Baha! May you rot in hell!"

The pot flew through the air and landed with a thud. The top flew off and rolled away. Suddenly, from out of the pot came the most brilliantly lit and glowing orbs of light Sean had ever seen. One by one, they came out of the pot, and as soon as they did, they flew as fast as anything ever flew, straight up into the darkness, forming the shape of a chair in the night sky, right next to the Big Dipper. All Sean could do was stand there and watch in utter amazement.

Composing himself in the days that followed, the only thing Sean could think to do, after he buried Cassie, was to visit Ishka Baha for himself.

As he approached the cabin, he heard a voice. He snuck through the trees, getting closer to the cabin, and saw the doctor sitting on a little stool on the porch, staring up at the sky and talking to no one, it seemed, but himself. Listening closely, and in horror, he heard Ishka Baha, who seemed to have lost his mind, speaking:

> "She's all mine, now-a-days, yessir! For it was me that gave her that teapot, fult o' 'the Barren sand,' knowin' what was gonna happen iffin' she did what me and the spoot told her to do, and iffin' she watered it with the spit on her finger just once. Mine ain't a body that wants to be doin' the woman sharin' with another body. Better to

> have her all mine, now-a-days, you know! And I see her, ev'ry night, I do, sittin' right there next to the Dipper, yessir! I'm still fond of callin' her Miss Cassie-O, and I stares, and stares, and stares …"

To this day, if you look up at the night sky of the Pine Barrens, just to the right of the Big Dipper, you will see a constellation in the shape of a chair, formed by a group of five bright stars. It doesn't take much to imagine the old doctor sitting on his little wooden stool somewhere, staring up at Cassie O'Paier as she sits there in the doctorin' chair. And from that night on, even to this day, women in the Pine Barrens who are ready and want to start a family are sternly warned: "Stay good and clear of Ishka Baha!"

Chakitty-Chikts

When you're out in the Pine Barrens, you'll notice how every sound you make seems to create a strange, hollow echo. Calling someone's name or the sound of someone chopping wood seems to echo and echo all through the forest, like magic. You'll also notice, at night, a very strange "Ch-Ch-Ch-Ch" sound coming from the trees now and again, here and there. Magic and strange? Not really. That, my friend, is the sound of the Chakitty-Chikts that live, only here, in the Barrens.

And this is their story.

A long, long time ago, even before the time of Christopher Columbus, Viking explorers came to North America. They got here in wooden boats called knorrs. The Vikings sailed and rowed these ships great distances across the oceans, until they finally reached our shores.

Now, the Vikings were unsure of what they would find when they arrived in the New World. They didn't know if there would be food to hunt and eat, so they brought as much fresh meat with them on their explorations as they could carry. One of their favorite meals was roasted troll. Yep, you heard me right—roasted troll!

These trolls were only about as tall as a man's thumb, but they were plump, sweet, and meaty, like shrimp. They looked like tiny monkeys, but they were covered with blonde, wavy hair from head to toe. They had one long, very pointy tooth that they used to poke holes in pine trees and then lick the sap that ran out.

Originally, the trolls had been gathered from the great pine forests of northern Norway, where they were known for a very special talent. Any sound that the trolls heard, they repeated instantly. And since there were thousands of trolls, each one living separately in one tree, next to the other, any sound at all would echo through the vast forest for miles and miles. This was how they warned one another of danger.

But the trolls had a weakness. For when a troll falls asleep, his snoring sounds like a loud *Cha*-kitty-*Chik* … *Cha*-kitty-*Chik* … *Cha*-kitty-*Chik*. That's how the Vikings were able to sneak up on and capture them. Their snoring gave them away.

The trolls were easy to raise, because all they ever ate were droplets of pine tree sap. They were a favorite on every Viking's dinner table and tasted particularly good served up with small, fire-roasted potatoes and washed down with plenty of mead, an alcoholic beverage made from honey. Several hundred trolls were kept in wooden pens on the ships during the Vikings' journey from Iceland to Greenland to Newfoundland and North America, ensuring that there would be plenty of fresh meat on the voyage and in the New World.

Now, on one such voyage, as the Vikings were unloading their ships, one of the pens full of trolls fell and broke open. Hundreds of trolls began running and scattering in every direction, with the angry Vikings trying to catch them. Trolls are quick and tricky, and adept at hiding under rocks and in trees, among other places, and

most of them did just that. They hid all day until it got dark, at which time the Vikings gave up looking for them and went back to their camp.

After the trolls were sure it was safe, they all gathered together, calling each other with their strange little clicking voices. They decided that the best thing for them to do was to head south, where it would be warmer, and as far away from the Vikings as they could get. So, that night, they all headed south, trying to escape the Vikings who would surely be looking for them come first light the next day.

The trolls ran and ran and ran all night long, until the sun started coming up. They were so tired they could barely take another step. They knew they had to rest and stay hidden, in case the Vikings were hunting for them. They were in a very thick pine forest.

Suddenly, the trolls were surrounded by a group of strange-looking people. These people wore beads and feathers, and had colorful markings on their faces. The trolls were frightened, but they were just too tired to run any more. One of the strange people looked down at the trolls and said, "I am Okanickon. We are the Nanticoke People who live here, in the Pine Lands. And we will not harm you."

The trolls were relieved that these people were friendly and decided to ask them if they would help keep them safe from the Vikings and let them live in the Pine Lands forever. In return, the trolls promised they would use their special talent of whispering everything they heard to help their hosts. This would be a boon to the Nanticokes when they were on a hunt, calling for their children, or assembling for any reason. It would warn them, too, whenever the Vikings, who didn't like the Nanticokes, were coming through the forest.

The Nanticokes and trolls agreed to protect one other and soon became great friends and allies. The trolls had found a new home where they weren't afraid of anything, with the notable exception of forest fires. There were thousands and thousands of pine trees for the trolls to live in, each filled with the sweet pinesap that sustained them. (There are those who swear that overfeeding by trolls resulted in hundreds and hundreds of acres of stunted trees known today as the "pygmy pines." But no one knows for sure.)

The Nanticokes gave a special name to the trolls—a name that described the sound they made when they were sleeping—and they became known forevermore as the Chakitty-Chikts.

To this very day, if you listen closely, you'll hear the Chakitty-Chikts live, snore, and whisper their echoes in the deep, dark forest we call the Pine Barrens.

Strange Towns of the Pine Barrens

If you were to look at an old map of the Pine Barrens, you might, indeed, find yourself wondering what could have happened in some of the towns that caused them to be known by such strange and mysterious names. Some of these places are still there, but most exist only in the legends of long, long ago.

But one still has to wonder: *How* did these towns get their names?

For instance, what in the world could have happened to the folks in DOUBLE TROUBLE?

What calamity could have taken place in MOUNT MISERY?

Who or what was everyone waiting for in LONG-A-COMING?

And what about OLD HALF-WAY? Where was it halfway *to* or halfway *from*?

What dastardly deed could have taken place in ONG'S HAT? (And where is the rest of old Mr. Ong?)

What do you suppose could have really been sold in BARGAIN-TOWN?

Perhaps we could ask BEVERLY, or SHIRLEY, or DOROTHY, or MARTHA, or ESTELLE, or FLORENCE. ... That is, if these gals aren't all off sunbathing in LOVELADIES.

What in hell could have happened in DUNKER?

And did it have anything at all to do with the WATER WITCH?

And why would anyone call a place CHANGE WATER? Was there something wrong with the water they had to begin with?

What were folks yelling from the banks of YAWP SHORE?

And what was poured into the river at SWEETWATER? (Perhaps a bad batch of CHEESEQUAKE?)

Might there have been some relationship between COCKED HAT, JENKINS NECK, and SKULLVILLE?

What do you suppose is buried in GREEN BANK and RED BANK? For that matter, why did the creek bed sink at LOWER BANK?

Exactly what kinds of goings-on were taking place in HOG WALLOW, HOG THIEF, CHICKEN BONE, CAT TAIL, and MAD HORSE? Not to mention BUCKSHUTEM and CROWS FOOT?

Who or what met their fate in DRAGSTOWN?

And whom were they chasing in STOP-THE-JADE-RUN?

Could the answer lie under SHELL PILE?

And one surely has to wonder if there is anything other than Captain Kidd's loot in PENNY POT.

Yes, my friend, there are many, many strange names of long-forgotten places and towns in the Pine Barrens of South Jersey. You'll need only an old map, a dark and misty night, and your imagination to conjure up the goings-on that gave these places their very special names.

But what *about* old Mr. Ong and his hat?

The Blessed Sands of South Jersey

Old-timers are fond of saying that the one sure way you can tell your clam chowder was made with real South Jersey clams, or that your cream of asparagus soup was made with real South Jersey asparagus, is by finding "it" in the bottom of your bowl. "It" is sand, a substance that is abundant in the region.

But the sand in South Jersey is not only abundant, it's *blessed*!

South Jersey sand gave birth to one of America's first successful industries: glassmaking. The early glassmakers found that the sand here is so pure in its natural state that it seems as though it's been washed clean of all impurities. It looks like pure white sugar, and there are mounds and mounds of this so-called sugar sand all over southern New Jersey—especially in the Pine Barrens.

So where did all of this pure white sand come from?

According to legend, the story goes like this.

The Almighty, in His wisdom, knew long, long ago that new settlers from all over the world would be coming to South Jersey to make new lives for themselves and their families. He also knew that Lucifer, the Devil, would be waiting for them, ready to throw his sin-greased monkey wrench into the works.

Just a few days before the first settlers arrived in South Jersey, The Almighty noticed that ol' Lucifer was lurking in and around the beaches, back bays, and swamps, waiting for the settlers. So, He called down to him.

"Lucifer!" said The Almighty.

"What is it now?" griped the Devil.

"I will make a deal with you for the lives and souls of these new settlers, if you promise to abide by the rules of the deal."

Now, Lucifer, with his foolish pride, believed that he could outsmart God in any deal or game, so he agreed to abide by the rules of The Almighty's deal.

"OK, I agree. What are the rules, then?" the Devil asked.

The Almighty smiled and said, "The rules are that you must pick up, wash, count, and stack, one by one, every single grain of sand in South Jersey before you can touch one single soul of the new settlers. You must start at the ocean, work your way through the Pine Barrens, and continue west to the Delaware River. When you are done, you may then have the souls of your choosing."

When the new settlers arrived, they saw the Devil picking up, washing, counting, and stacking grain upon grain of sand on the beach. Each time the Devil had stacked a pile of sand high, he would call up to The Almighty and say, "This one is done!" (With his accent, "done" sounded like "dune," which explains how the piles of sand at the shore came to be called *dunes*.)

The settlers would laugh and snicker as they watched old Lucifer working endlessly, which made him so mad that great amounts of intense heat would radiate from his body. This is why, to this day, one can get quite a nasty burn on the beach even when the sky is overcast.

If you're ever traveling through the Pine Barrens on one of the many long, sandy roads, be forewarned, friend. Trickster that he is, the Devil has laid quite a few sugar-sand traps along those roads, and it's been many a sad traveler indeed who has had his horse or his vehicle sink from sight in Pine Barrens sand.

To this day, old Lucifer is still counting, stacking, and washing sand in South Jersey. That's why, every now and again, you'll find a mound of sand in the Pine Barrens that seems strangely out of place, or a sand dune on a beach where there wasn't one the week before. And in many Piney homes, you can still find fruit jars filled with sand under each bed in the house, the belief being that the Devil must count *each and every* grain of sand, one at a time, between dusk and dawn, before he can do any harm to the soul layin' in the bed. Some folks swear that the reason they stopped making so much glass in South Jersey was to stop using up all the sand in order to ensure the old Devil would never finish his eternal chore.

Who's to say, but one thing is for certain: The day will probably never come when the Devil finally finishes washing, counting, and stacking the blessed sands of South Jersey.

Lure of the Loveladies

Folks have met their fate in and around the Pine Barrens in some strange and untimely ways over the years. Hidden, out-of-place bogs, runaway stagecoaches, plundering and marauding highwaymen, ghostly winged creatures, and, yes, even fish, have all brought an end to hapless, helpless victims of this very special, albeit sometimes dangerous place.

Consider the story of one unlucky soul down the shore.

He saw it from the top of the September Road jetty. A *gold coin*. Lying there, in the surf, in about 3 feet of water. A *gold* coin!

He'd been walking north, along the beach in Loveladies, a small South Jersey seashore town on the north end of Long Beach Island—or LBI, as the natives call it. He was about halfway between the September Road and Pompano Road jetties when he noticed a school of bluefish in a feeding frenzy near the Pompano side. It seemed the school was slowly drifting south, toward September Road. He figured they must be chasing mullet, or menhaden, that were being driven by the waves into the rocks that made up the jetties. Turning around, he ran over to the September Road jetty, hoping to get a better look at the school of blues.

He was an avid fisherman who frequently fished off the jetties of Loveladies and other LBI towns. Now he was kicking himself for not having brought his fishing gear with him, though it was early in the season. The blues didn't usually show up this early.

Loveladies, and the entire north end of LBI, was one of his favorite places. Overgrown with pine, holly, emerald juniper, bayberry, beach plum, and other plants and shrubs native to the shore, it was here, he thought, that the last finger of the Pine Barrens had poked as far east as it could.

Walking out onto the September jetty, he looked at the expanse of water between where he stood and the Pompano jetty, some 500 yards away. The school of bluefish was nowhere to be seen, but it was at this moment, looking down into the surf that was crashing onto the rocks, that he spied the coin. It was a shining, brilliant orb. It seemed to light up the water all around where it laid in the sand. It appeared almost electric, he thought, the way it glowed in the sun.

He'd pegged the coin as a relic from one of the hundreds of ships that had wrecked off the coast of LBI over the centuries. It was about 5 feet from the side of the jetty, in about 3 feet of water.

The tide was coming in, so he knew he had to act quickly. He had to have that coin. He wasn't just a fisherman, after all—he was a treasure hunter who had combed the Jersey shore with his metal detector for many years, looking for the treasure that often washed up on its beaches, especially after storms.

He climbed down the granite rocks that made up the jetty. They were slippery and dangerous, and he knew that if his foot got caught in a crevasse he could easily twist an ankle, if not break a leg. A powerful wave crashed into the jetty, soaking him from head to toe.

Stepping carefully off the jetty and into the water, he gripped a large rock with one hand as he bent over to try to grab the gold coin. It was just out of reach. Letting go of the rock, he took two steps and reached down into the water. The coin was in his hand!

It was beautiful. Heavy. Shining and brilliant. A solid gold Spanish doubloon. A once-in-a-lifetime find, and it was all his. Finally! *Gold*!

As he turned back toward the jetty, he felt his foot sink into the soft sand. As he tried to free one foot, the other sank as well. The more he tried to move, the deeper he sank. A wave of panic washed over him. He let out a yell, but as far as he could see, there was no one in sight who might hear him. The tide was coming in with a vengeance, and the waves that had been breaking over his waist were now rising to his chest and shoulders. He began screaming in earnest, but his screams were lost in the sound of the pounding surf.

Suddenly, not 50 feet from where he stood stuck in the sand, he saw the water "boiling"—the telltale sign of a school of bluefish in a feeding frenzy. They were drifting in toward him. As the waves began to break over his head, he gasped for air, screaming each time his face broke the water.

He felt something nip his hand and then the frenzied movement of the school all around him. Thousands of bluefish, making the water churn.

As the water rose over his head, he could no longer catch and hold a breath. He felt the nips of teeth coming fast and furious now. Just before he lost consciousness, he looked down to see the gold coin slip out of his hand and drift down to the sea bed. It glistened and shimmered as it descended, and then faded from view as his life dissolved in the roiling surf.

When the crimson waters cleared, the great bluefish, the largest one in the school, swam to the gold coin and quickly picked it up between its jaws. It turned, and with a powerful thrust of its tail, caught up with the rest of the school. The bluefish headed south, toward the Sea Pines Road jetty, just as an old man and his plump wife reached the water's edge.

The school hung back, just offshore, as the great bluefish slipped to within a few feet of the jetty. Gently dropping the coin, it swam away … and waited.

"Look!" the old man said excitedly to his wife as he climbed down the rocks of the jetty. "A *gold coin*!"

The Hangin' Tree

Memory is sometimes a strange thing and can be especially strange in the Pine Barrens. Some things get remembered, and some things don't. What's more, some things *have* a memory, or so it seems, that shouldn't, or supposedly *couldn't* have one.

You wouldn't think a flock of buzzards could have a memory about an event that took place more than 200 years ago and return every year on the same day to commemorate it. But that's the case. And it continues to this day, every August 28, at the Hangin' Tree of Hangin'emton.

A long time ago in South Jersey, men and, every once in awhile, women, were hanged after being convicted of certain crimes. Robbery, rape, murder, and the forgery of public securities were some of the more than 200 crimes that were punishable with death by hanging.

Hangin'emton, located in just about the center of South Jersey's Pine Barrens, was known for its glassmaking factory, or "works," and for the huge stands of pine, cedar, and oak that surrounded and supported the bustling town with fuel for its glass furnaces.

It was also known as a place for what folks in the Pine Barrens called "the Hangin' Tree." Hangin'emton got its name because it was *the* town where they were hangin' 'em. People, that is. Convicted criminals.

Because of the town's central location and the fact that it had the only courthouse with a sitting judge in all of the Pine Barrens region, most criminals arrested by local sheriffs and marshals elsewhere in the Jersey countryside were brought to Hangin'emton for trial. If convicted of a hangin' offense, they were held in the Hangin'emton jail until hanging day, which was held once a year on August 28.

Short of escaping or having their convictions overturned, which rarely ever happened, and after spending varying amounts of time in jail, depending on what month they were convicted and remanded to the jail, the condemned convicts were only a short buckboard wagon-ride away from their "big swing."

The Hangin' Tree stood some 75 feet tall and was located where Second Road intersected with Weymouth Road, a couple miles south of "downtown" Hangin'emton. It was one of the only Rock Maples anyone could recall ever seeing in the Pine Barrens and certainly the tallest. It stood out like a sore thumb in the lush greenness of the pine, cedar, and oak forest not only due to its enormity, but because it was dark gray, nearly black in color, and graveyard *dead*. Its branches reached up into the sky like a handful of bony, arthritically gnarled fingers. There wasn't a pleasant thing about it. Folks say it even *smelled* awful. In short, that tree seemed to have been placed there for the one purpose it *did* serve: death.

No one ever remembered seeing even a leaf on the Hangin' Tree, ever. In fact, no one ever remembered seeing *anything* on it—not birds, squirrels, moss, fungi, or anything else that was alive other than the wriggling, grunting, hooded, and soon-to-be-dead convicts

who wound up strung up and hanging from one of its branches every August 28. And except for that day, when most of Hangin'emton's townsfolk showed up for the annual hanging, folks went out of their way to use different routes and paths so as not to have to pass anywhere near the Hangin' Tree. The story around town was that if one were to just walk through its *shadow*, some of it might stick on you and kill you.

In 1750, a 22-year-old blacksmith by the name of Alan Hartigan moved to Hangin'emton from Connecticut. Hartigan was a hard-working man who kept mostly to himself, staying busy and trying to grow his small, fledgling business. He had no wife as of yet but was intent on finding one "here in the Jerseys" and starting a family once he securely established his business in town.

Soon after moving in, Alan met Hope Gagonhardt at a church social. Hope was a beautiful, statuesque young woman of 20 whose father, Euell B. Gagonhardt—his friends called him "Yul-be"—was the presiding judge in Hangin'emton. Charming, gracious, and well-educated for the times, Hope was thought of locally as the closest thing to a debutante the Pine Barrens could or would ever produce. "Fit for a king … or at least a judge!" her father would cackle boastfully of his only child, Hope, to anyone in earshot.

Yul-be, on the other hand, was anything *but* charming, gracious, and well-educated. To call him a cheating, corrupt, portly slob would have been an understatement. But that's what he was—a bully who'd gotten his appointment to the bench for the right price and from the right place in the governor's office up in Trenton.

Many folks swore that the governor had appointed Yul-be just to keep him busy in the Pine Barrens and out of his hair.

Yul-be named his daughter "Hope" because, as she was being born, her mother, Octavia, suddenly and for no apparent reason, stopped breathing and died, and it was thought that the baby would succumb to asphyxiation. But the doctor and midwives quickly separated the child from the umbilical cord, and Hope survived.

As the relationship between Hope and Hartigan deepened, Hope's father grew more and more concerned. He had always wanted someone high up on the social ladder for his daughter; a common blacksmith from Connecticut wasn't at all what he had in mind. A doctor, a lawyer, or perhaps a wealthy plantation or factory owner was more in line with his expectations for the man who would marry Hope.

During dinner one night, Yul-be began a conversation concerning the cotillion ball he wanted to plan for his daughter.

"But, Daddy, I don't want a 'coming out' party," Hope said. "I don't wish to be introduced and put on display. I am quite happy with my station in life as your daughter, and as the future Mrs. Alan Hartigan."

The judge nearly choked on the mouthful of clam stew he was trying to swallow. "What is this talk of the future Mrs. Alan Hartigan?" he sputtered, coughing clam chunks and potato into his napkin. "You're barely out of your knickers, and I'll hear none of this!"

"Alan is a good and honorable and hardworking man, Daddy, and I love him!" Hope said, the tears welling up in her eyes. "He wants to marry me as soon as his business becomes a little more profitable and family-worthy."

Yul-be knew that although he was upset and seething inside at the thought of his daughter marrying a blacksmith, there was little use in arguing with a woman in love—never mind that the woman was his only child, his pride and joy. He knew a carefully laid-out plan would need to be formulated and acted upon, one in which he could have the blacksmith somehow eliminated from the picture while keeping the deed hidden forever from Hope.

Backing away from the argument and thereby easing his daughter's distress and diffusing the situation at the dinner table, the judge composed himself, smiled, and said calmly, "Let us speak of such things later, darling, after I've gotten to know your Mr. Hartigan a little better. I'm sure he is a fine man, in that he's captured *your* heart. Perhaps we'll arrange a luncheon meeting for all concerned, in lieu of the cotillion?"

"Oh, yes, Daddy, that would be wonderful, and I know you will think admirably of Alan!"

The judge had to move fast, and he knew it. No blacksmith from anywhere was going to marry his daughter, and marriage was clearly where this courtship was heading. He thought and thought and thought, and then devised a plan to vanquish Alan Hartigan.

With the annual hanging just 2 days away, the judge would arrange to have Hartigan captured and hanged in the place of the one man who had been condemned this year and was being held in the Hangin'emton jail. "This couldn't have worked out better, only one man to swing this year," the judge thought to himself as he secretly walked over to see the town's constable, jailkeeper, and executioner, Steven Connors. Yul-be and Connors had grown up together and were the best of friends. Connors was a string-bean-shaped man—"as stupid and bad with a pistol as he was skinny" is what folks in Hangin'emton said about him.

"Steven," said the judge as he sat down on Connors's desk at the jailhouse, "I need you to do a favor for me."

"Anything for you, Yul-be, you know that. What is it?"

"I want you to arrest that blacksmith, Alan Hartigan, and keep him here in the jail, all nice and covered up and quiet-like, out of the public's eye until the day after tomorrow, the 28th—hangin' day—then hang *him* instead of that murderer in that cell over there."

Connors looked at the judge with eyes as wide as saucers for a few moments, and then said, simply, "Uh, OK, Yul-be, but what the hell do you have against that blacksmith, and what the hell do I do with Stanton?" He motioned to the cell where the sleeping, condemned Michael Stanton lay, unaware of his unfolding and changing fate.

"Hartigan's after my Hope is what the hell I have against him!" the judge shot back in a whispered shout. "As for him," he nodded toward Stanton, "hell, just shoot him out in the woods and bury him. What's the damn difference *how* he dies? He's dying, one way or the other."

The judge left the jailhouse knowing Connors would carry out his wishes.

Sure enough, the next day the whole town was talkin' about the blacksmith, Alan Hartigan, and how he'd just up and left during the night, going back to Connecticut, explaining in a note left on his door that he'd had all he could take of life in the Pine Barrens. Hope was inconsolable. She stayed locked in her bedroom, crying for hours on end.

The following morning, hangin' day, broke clear. All morning long, folks traveled through town, down along Main Street, then turned left on Second Road, and headed south for the three miles or so it took to get to the Hangin' Tree. Some rode in horse-drawn wagons, some came on horseback, and others simply walked. Hangings were huge, gala events back in the day, and nearly everyone in town attended, many with picnic baskets loaded with luncheon fare.

It seemed that everyone in town was there, with the exception of the grieving Hope Gagonhardt.

Around 11:30 AM, Connors arrived in the buckboard with the condemned prisoner, already leg-shackled, bound, gagged, hooded, and covered from head to waist in a burlap sack wrapped 'round and 'round with a tight, thick rope.

Connors led the prisoner slowly through the crowd toward the platform that had been built next to the hangin' tree. The prisoner could be heard groaning and grunting in a high, ear-piercing pitch, trying to be heard over the shouts and jeers of the crowd, but his words were unintelligible due to the gag and the hood.

Connors had a hell of a time getting the prisoner through the crowd and up the steps of the platform, due to the way the prisoner was dragging his feet and twitching and turning his body. Finally, Connors got him to the top, where Judge Euell B. Gagonhardt was waiting. The entire scene, Connors noticed as a chill crawled up his back, was being observed by a flock of black buzzards that had perched themselves on the upper branches of the hangin' tree.

Yul-be raised both arms and waved his hands up and down to quiet the hundreds of spectators who stood or sat there before him, watching and waiting for the "big swing" to happen. When the crowd noise had quieted to an acceptable level, the judge turned to face the prisoner and spoke in a loud, booming voice. "Michael Stanton, you've been found guilty of the murder of Snorey Mortimer by a jury of your peers and sentenced to hang by the neck until you're dead. Do you have any last words?"

The prisoner grunted and groaned as loud as he could in those high pitches, twisting and contorting his body as Connors tried to hold him steady. The judge put a cupped hand to his ear, turned his head slightly toward the crowd, and yelled, "What? I can't *heeeeaaarrr* you …" as he broke into a huge belly laugh, rejoicing inwardly that he would soon be rid of this damned blacksmith.

The crowd erupted in frenzied laughter and whistles as they shouted in unison, "Drop him! Drop him!"

Again, the judge shouted, "I can't *heeeaaarrrr* you …"

The crowd continued to whistle and hoot and shout "Drop him! Drop him!" Connors lowered the noose over the head of the prisoner, tightened it, and then placed the knot next to the prisoner's neck. Backing away from the condemned, whose knees were starting to buckle as he continued groaning and grunting, Connors looked at the judge. The judge nodded, and Connors pulled back on the handle that opened the trap door in the floor of the platform on which the prisoner was standing.

The prisoner fell through the hole. The rope straightened and went taught. The body bounced with a sudden jerk back up about a foot, slacking the rope momentarily, and then going taught again as it hanged there, swinging slightly back and forth and twisting. But even after the long fall through the trap door and the horrific jerk that ensued as he reached the end of the rope that was *supposed* to snap his neck like a twig and kill him instantly, the prisoner continued kicking and groaning. Not a buzzard moved from its perch on the tree.

The crowd had been laughing, cheering, and jeering, but now grew quiet as one, two, then three minutes passed. The man was still alive, struggling, kicking, and groaning.

Connors looked at Yul-be. "Now what?" he asked.

The judge motioned to two onlookers in the crowd, shouting, "You two. Come up here, quick, and lend a hand!"

When the two men reached the top of the steps, the judge said, "Pull him back up through that hole and drop him again."

The crowd was falling more and more silent, with some actually calling for the prisoner to be set free, since he'd beaten the noose the first time. Others, mostly women and children, began leaving the area. Not only did they not like what they were witnessing, but a storm was approaching from the northwest.

"Hurry up and yank him up here, for Christ's sake!" yelled Yul-be to Connors and the two men who were pulling the rope up through the hole.

The men pulled the still-wriggling, groaning, and grunting prisoner up through the trap door, moved him aside, then closed and latched the door again. They stood the prisoner back on the trap door, reset the noose and knot, and looked over to the judge.

"Do it!" Yul-be yelled.

Once again Connors pulled the handle, dropping the prisoner and again snapping his neck. And, once again, the prisoner fought, kicked, and groaned in that high-pitched, muffled screech. One minute went by, then two, and the prisoner continued to kick and scream. Death simply would not come.

The crowd was shouting for the prisoner to be cut down and freed. Men were threatening to hang the judge if he didn't let the prisoner go or do something immediately. Off in the distance, thunder could be heard from the approaching storm. From the upper branches of the Hangin' Tree, the black buzzards looked down in silence.

As the crowd began moving closer to the hanging, twitching prisoner, Yul-be and Connors rushed down the steps. There was no way they could let the prisoner be unhooded and identified, because it was Alan Hartigan under that hood rather than convicted killer Michael Stanton. They'd be hanged themselves if anyone discovered what they'd done, not to mention the agony that would be inflicted on Hope.

As the skies opened up and a torrential rain began to fall, Yul-be pulled the revolver from Connors' holster and shot the prisoner one time in the head. Mercifully, the body immediately stopped twitching. "And that's the end of *that*!" the judge intoned as he handed the revolver back to Connors.

The crowd was dispersing now in every direction, with people rushing to get back to their homes and out of the blinding summer thunderstorm that had hit the town so quickly. Yet even now, in the driving wind and rain, not a buzzard left its station in the Hangin' Tree.

"After you get me into town, I want you to come back here to cut that sum-bitch down and bury him," the judge said to Connors. The two rode back to town as fast as the horses could pull the old buckboard wagon up Second Road. Arriving at the jail, they went inside to sign the death certificate and dry off.

As the judge and Connors walked through the jailhouse door, they were greeted by a sight that nearly dropped both of them where they stood. It was none other than a very-much-alive Michael Stanton—the same Michael Stanton who was originally supposed to hang for the murder of Snorey Mortimer, and the same Michael Stanton whom Connors had taken out in the woods the night before and *thought* he'd shot dead. Now, Stanton was pointing a double barrel over/under shotgun at them.

"Come on in, boys, and sit down," commanded the smiling Stanton. "I've been 'spectin' ya's!"

The two men, staring dumbfounded at Stanton, shuffled over to the chairs and sat down. The three men just looked at each other for a while, Stanton smiling, Connors vomiting, and the judge shaking his head in disbelief.

Finally, Stanton spoke. "You two are really a pair of half-asses. I listened to your whole plan last night while I was pretending to be asleep there yon," he said, motioning to the cell across the room.

Yul-be and Connors looked at one other, sighing and shaking their heads as Stanton continued. "When you took me out to those woods last night, Stevie-boy, and shot me, you were still the same lousy shot you always been, and you didn't make sure I was dead. Hah! As you can see, I ain't. Grazed my ear is all you done!"

The judge looked at Connors and yelled, "You damn fool! Why didn't you check to make sure you killed him?"

"After you left me layin' there in the woods and were headed over to Hartigan's," Stanton continued, "I went over to *your* house, Judge, while you were in town tryin' to drink it dry, and captured me that gal that was bawlin' up a storm in that room upstairs in your house. Know a girl named Hope, Judge?" Stanton burst out laughing.

"No!" the judge screamed.

"Oh, yes, sir!" laughed Stanton. "Hope and I waited just around the corner in the back there, her not havin' any choice in the matter, what with my knife to her throat and bein' all tied up, you see, and watched ol' Stevie-boy sneak the blacksmith in here real secret-like, or so you thought. Thought you were gonna hang him instead of me, eh?"

Again, Stanton let out a huge, bellowing laugh, then continued. "You wrapped, gagged, and packaged him up real good, and left him in that cell all night. What you didn't do, because you thought he was wrapped up tight like a stuffed cabbage leaf, was lock that cell door. I left Hope tied up out back there, and I came in here and told Hartigan about the big plan you boys had, and how his girl was in on it, unwrapped him, and gave him the choice of a bullet or to skeedaddle back up Connecticut way, which I guess he's doin' right now."

Yul-be and Connors just looked at each other in disbelief. Then the judge turned to Stanton and shouted, "If Hartigan is on his way back to Connecticut, then who in hell is swingin' from the Hangin' Tree?"

"It's your gal Hope, Judgie-Boy. The apple of your eye! She was a big, strong girl, and she fought me tough, but I finally wrapped 'er up in Hartigan's swingin' suit after I chased *him* outta here and brought *her* in, ropes, gags, burlap, and all. Nobody ever knew the difference—not even you, Connors! You carried her to the Hangin' Tree thinkin' it was Hartigan, and you, Judge, hanged your own daughter *twice* then blew her brains out, all because you didn't like her boyfriend, who you wanted to hang in my place. Hah, Hah, Hah!"

They say Judge Gagonhardt and Steven Connors screamed for a long time before that 12-gauge over/under went off that day, sending both of them instantly into the great unknown. Stanton got away, was rearrested, and then was hanged some months later for horse thieving in Virginia and told the whole Hope Gagonhardt story again before he died. No one ever saw or heard from or knew what had become of Alan Hartigan, nor does anyone know who hung the sign next to the Hangin' Tree that reads "Here Hope Swings Eternal."

That was the last time anyone was ever hanged from that tree. They've tried, down through the years, over and over again, to cut it down, but they've yet to find a saw that can cut through the wood. Folks have tried burning it and blasting it, but to no avail. The tree just stands there. Dead.

Hangin'emton, being not only a tongue-twister to pronounce, but, and even more so, having such a reviled, morbid reputation, was renamed "Hammonton" in an all-out effort to finally shed the ghastly memories of that day. But every August 28, beginning with the day of that last hanging, right up to present day, a flock of black buzzards gathers silently in that tree at the corner of Second and Weymouth roads … watching, waiting, remembering, and possibly commemorating the day Hope Gagonhardt died on the Hangin' Tree.

The Hole in the Pine Barrens

Down through the ages, passed on from generation to generation, from fathers and mothers to sons and daughters, are the seemingly countless legends, stories, and songs about the people and places of the Pine Barrens. The Barrens is one of the richest and well-known places in the country, and even the world, "where strange things happen." All the life that can happen, and even what can't, happens here in the Pines.

One such legend deals with the story of how the Blue Hole, a body of water in the southwestern corner of the Pine Barrens, came to be. Science has tried to explain it away as a lateral column of ice, or what's called a pingo, that was formed during the last Ice Age and then melted, leaving a bottomless pit of year-round 50-degree, ice-blue water. Other scientists have claimed that it is the result of a meteor strike, as evidenced by the high banks that surround the Blue Hole and give it the appearance of a water-filled crater.

Over the years, scores of folks, from area locals to scientists arriving from afar, have tried to measure the depth of the Blue Hole, using cables, ropes, poles, sticks, and even scuba gear, in an effort to prove or disprove its bottomlessness. The jury is still out, as results "proving" both theories are many.

It's been rumored that the Jersey Devil lurks in and about the Blue Hole, no doubt enjoying a refreshing dunk in the crystal-blue water now and then, most likely whilst planning another county or statewide sojourn like the one in 1909 that he's so famous for. Some say if you go swimming in the Blue Hole, old "JD" will grab you from where he's waiting in the depths and pull you under with him. It's said that there are whirly pools and strange "gravity-dropped" currents in the Blue Hole, and, for years and years, parents in the area have forbidden their children to swim in it, or, for that matter, to go anywhere near it.

And then, there's another story about how the Blue Hole came to be.

It started as a mean joke—a trick played on a young Native American lad. They say his name was Tecototata (*Tee*-ko-too-*ta*-ta) and that he was one of the Lenni-Lenape who used to live in and around the Pine Barrens before the white men came. He was known simply as "Teko" to his family and so-called friends.

As the story goes, Teko was not the brightest star in the Pine Barrens sky, but he was true and fair of heart. He would go out of his way to gain favor with the members of his family and tribe by doing whatever was asked of him, never questioning or arguing too much about it.

One day, a group of braves spotted Teko standing alone, fishing for his family's evening supper in the river. They hatched a nasty plan to trick him into doing something that everyone would laugh at him for trying to attempt. They drew a 100-foot-wide circle on the forest floor with a stick near the river, made up a story, and approached Teko.

"Teko, the Elders have decided that you are to take all the dirt out of that hole over there and throw it into the river. The dirt you

remove from the hole will wash downstream and create more land for us."

Teko turned, startled, and faced the braves who were standing there. "What hole do you speak of? I see no hole," he said, looking in the woods behind them.

"Of *course* you don't see the hole, Teko. It is filled with dirt. You are to dig until that hole is empty!"

The braves walked Teko over to the circle that they'd drawn on the forest floor.

"Do you see the hole now, Teko?" one of the braves asked.

"I see it, I think. Yes, I do. That is a large hole to empty!"

"You must start at once, Teko," they said. "The Elders want this done quickly!"

"But how will I know when the hole is empty?" Teko asked.

"When there is no more dirt in it!" the braves yelled together.

And with that, the braves ran off into the forest, leaving Teko alone with the two large clam shells he was to use for digging.

Teko dug. He dug, and he dug, and he dug some more. He'd pile the dirt from the hole on a deerskin he had planned to use to bring his fish back in, then drag it about 50 yards to the river and dump it in. Hour after hour, he dug and emptied, dug and emptied. For days he dug and emptied, but he still couldn't empty the hole of its dirt.

Members of Teko's tribe who did not know of the ruse were becoming increasingly worried as to his whereabouts. Teko had never been gone for such a long time, and his parents were frantic. Finally, the Elders called a noon council meeting to discuss the now weeklong missing Teko and what was to be done to find him. Near the end of the meeting, after the search parties were made up and coordinated, one of the braves, Onoquay, who'd been party to the trick played on Teko, could take the guilt no more and started crying. He confessed to what had happened to Teko and why he was now missing.

The men of the tribe all ran toward the river but were stopped in their tracks by a huge, incredibly blue, 100-foot-wide pool of water. It seemed perfectly round and was ice cold to the touch. It was in the precise location where the braves had drawn their circle on the forest floor a week earlier to trick Teko.

In emptying the hole of dirt, Teko had tapped into the Lake of Life—the hidden body of fresh water that circles the Earth, even below the lakes, streams, and oceans. Teko had emptied so much dirt from the hole into the river that new, virgin land had been created, and now, the great "Salt Water Lake" was some 30 miles farther away from where it had been before Teko started digging.

The chief of the tribe, Nesqochague, called for the braves who were responsible for Teko's disappearance as well as, evidently, the new water and land formations. He spoke to them, saying, "You have caused an unnatural thing with your trickery. Cursed forever are these waters now. As cold as ice shall they stay for all time, so as to reflect the cold of your hearts toward one who trusted you."

He ordered them to enter the water and dive down to the bottom to retrieve Teko's body. The braves all entered the water together. They were only a few feet from the bank when they all screamed in horror, saying that they saw Teko in the depths and were being drawn under the water by him. They quickly disappeared under the surface and were never seen or heard from again.

People continue to disappear in the Blue Hole to this day. And the dirt that Teko emptied from the hole that washed down the Great Egg Harbor River today forms Atlantic and Cape May counties, having created some of the sandiest, yet richest farmland anywhere in the world. It is said that this soil, thanks to Teko, makes Jersey tomatoes and asparagus the most flavorful on Earth.

Tecototata? The Jersey Devil? There's no way to unravel the mystery, but here's hoping that all the holes you find in your life are full, and that you know only the true and fair of heart, love the ones you trust, and trust the ones you love.

Jersey Deviled Clams

Have you ever seen a Jersey Deviled Clam? Myself, I'm *always* lookin' for Jersey Deviled Clams. They're very hard to find, but when you do finally find one, you'll agree, it was well worth the lookin' for … and well worth the waitin' for.

What *is* a Jersey Deviled Clam, you're askin'? Well, according to the legend, the story goes like this.

All during the many years and years that the Jersey Devil has been haunting South Jersey, one of his favorite foods has always been fresh, sweet, tender clams. Clams can be found in many places throughout this area, and they were, and remain to be, one of the main food staples that the people who live in the Pines thrive on. In fact, clamming is still a large and important industry in South Jersey.

Now, the Jersey Devil, they say, finds his clams during the night along the deserted beaches in the back bays and salt marshes of South Jersey, and gathers them in one of his huge wings that acts like a basket. He then sneaks back into the Barrens, where he sits in front of his pile of clams and enjoys them as a nice, tasty supper. But it's the very special way that the Jersey Devil opens his clams, and the mistake he makes every now and then, that produces the very rare and valuable Jersey *Deviled* Clam.

You see, the Jersey Devil can't open his clams like people do, because he has hooves like a horse and claws instead of hands and nimble fingers. So, what he does is breathe just the right amount of his fiery breath onto the clams, and they open up, steamed to perfection, and ready to eat. However, every once in a great while the Jersey Devil breathes a little too much onto a clam—probably because he's real hungry and in a hurry—and it melts the sand that is found in all South Jersey clams and some of the shell. This forms a blob of beautifully colored South Jersey glass.

Because this turns the tender, sweet clam into a rock-hard, inedible piece of glass, the Jersey Devil simply throws it aside, where it waits and waits to be discovered by someone like you or me.

Some folks say that, back in the old days, when oysters were as plentiful as clams in South Jersey, it was this opening process the Jersey Devil used on his oysters that caused pearls to be made. Oysters, unfortunately, have all but disappeared from the waters of South Jersey, so these days the ol' Jersey Devil concentrates mainly on the ever-abundant clams.

Jersey Deviled Clams can be found still in the clam shell or all by themselves, simply lying there on the ground. They can be found in the woods of the Pine Barrens or along the many rivers and streams in the Pines, and along the beaches of the back bays and marshes. It all depends where the Jersey Devil was when he was trying to have his supper.

These "deviled" clams come in several different colors, depending on how hot the fire was when he opened a particular clam. Some are light blue, which means the fire wasn't too hot. Others are a darker blue or green, which means it was pretty hot. Others are darn near black, which means it was getting very, very hot. And still others are red, which means the Devil's fire was terribly hot, and he was probably very, *very* hungry and impatient.

South Jersey's Native American tribes of long ago made beautiful jewelry with the Deviled Clams they found. Many an old Indian was known to believe that the Jersey Devil would never harm anyone wearing or possessing a Jersey Deviled Clam, and so they were often kept in Native American huts to ward off unwanted visits. They were said to bring good luck and were prized possessions of all who owned them.

Sometimes the clams were traded for different goods between the tribes, and, later, between the tribes and new settlers, who had things the Indians had never seen before—guns for hunting and European tools and medicines. Jersey Deviled Clams were, and still are, very beautiful and valuable, indeed.

Have *you* ever seen a Jersey Deviled Clam?

Myself, I'm *always* lookin' for Jersey Deviled Clams.

The Deadbus

Stagecoaches have been a part of life in the Pine Barrens dating from the earliest days of European settlement. So many of the roads and famous intersections we use today got their start long, long ago as stagecoach runs, stop-offs, and boarding points. It seems that all the legends and stories in and about South Jersey, sooner or later, get around to having something to do with a stagecoach.

And stagecoaches are *still* running through the Pine Barrens after all these years. However, these days, they run along "cement trails" instead of the sugar-sand roads of yesteryear. We call them buses, and these buses have their own legends and stories to tell.

One such is the Deadbus.

I saw it tonight, drivin' down the pike, through the Pines, heading to Atlantic City.

The Deadbus. Number 8802. That's what "they" called it. The Deadbus.

I remember that Deadbus. I know that Deadbus. More intimately than I care to.

"They" were the guys I used to work with at transit a few years back, in 2005. We were "hostlers"—the guys who fuel, clean (inside and out), and wash buses for transit. Day in and day out. 24/7/365. Every bus. Every day.

I remember the first night I saw the Deadbus. It was my third night on the job. The old hands on my crew, the 4–12 shift, were tellin' me, the new and only white guy, about "blood buses" and "vomit buses," "needle buses" and "boogitty buses," and warnin' me to be careful of all four.

Blood buses were buses that came into the garage with wet blood in and/or on the seats or floors. Blood gets on buses in a variety of ways. Fights. Suicides. Menstruating women. Blood buses are dangerous in that the blood might carry any one of several harmful infectious diseases. That's why there's an endless supply of latex gloves in the lunchroom in the garage.

It goes without saying what's on a vomit bus. And a needle bus is pretty self-explanatory, too. Riders shooting up drugs and leaving their needles behind. More than one hostler, I was told, got hepatitis from being poked by a junkie's needle that was down between a seat and back cushion. That's why there's an endless supply of wooden paint-stirring sticks in the lunchroom next to the latex gloves. Use the stick to fish out what's between the cushions, I was told.

A "boogitty bus" is where the hookers perform their services when nowhere else is available. They and their johns leave behind prophylactics, undergarments, and fluids of all kinds from "gettin' some o' dat boogitty," I was told.

But that night, when Bus 8802 rolled in, all of a sudden it seemed like the rest of the training session regarding "danger" buses didn't matter. Not the blood bus. Not the vomit bus. Not the needle bus. And not the boogitty bus. Number 8802—the Deadbus—was all that mattered.

And none of my co-workers wanted any part of it.

They all looked at me, suddenly announcing that they were going on break, and told me I had to service 8802 myself.

Fuel it. Clean it, inside and out. Run it through the automatic bus wash at the end of the bay, and then go park it out in the garage area.

The garage area is a huge, three-acre terminal-looking affair that houses all 1,200 transit buses when they're not on the road. It's dark and weird back in there. Lots of buses and lots of windows. Dark windows. Windows that people look out of all day as they're riding the bus. Walking through there, in and around all those empty buses with all those empty windows, can get … well, you just have to get used to it. And used to the quiet.

What the hell did I care? I did it. Fueled it. Checked the tires, oil, coolant, and washer fluid. Checked the running lights, wipers, and mirrors. Went inside. Made sure there were no heroin needles lyin' on any seats. Made sure there was no suicide blood on the floors or wino vomit—things you generally find on buses that run between Camden and Atlantic City. Sometimes you find bodies, living and/or dead, on buses as you service them. People fall asleep and wind up at the garage. Or choose the bus to kill themselves on. We find 'em, one way or the other. I guessed that they had found somebody dead on this bus, 8802, and that was how it got its name.

As I drove 8802 through the washer machine and turned to park it in the garage, I saw a driver sitting in a chair at the end of the washer bay. He was wearing one of the older-style transit driver uniforms. He waved at me, looking up from a book he was holding in his hands, and I tooted the horn at him. I drove the bus to garage

"F," all the way at the end of the building, parked it, and shut it down.

As I walked away and back toward the service island, I thought I heard something. I stopped and looked back at 8802. Yes, I *had* heard something!

It was a kid, for Chrissakes! A little girl, and she was crying. *My God!* How had I missed her? She must have been left on the bus—maybe curled up under a seat. I felt horrible that I'd missed her and ran back toward 8802.

As I opened the door and climbed up the four steps, I heard laughing coming from the back of the bus. I switched the interior lights on, and, sitting there, almost all the way back, was the driver I had seen near the washer machine, reading a storybook to a little black girl. She was laughing at the story. They both looked up at me and smiled.

I ran as fast as I could, back to the service island, completely freaked out. "*Yo! Yo!* There's a driver with a kid!"

The guys in my crew came out of the lunchroom slowly. They were staring at me. I stood there, just about frozen and freaked out at the same time.

"You all right?" asked Gussy, the senior hostler on my crew.

"Hell, *no*, I ain't all right!" I said, shaking. "There's a friggin' driver with a kid on 8802 reading a goddamned book!"

"No, there ain't, man. Not really," Gussy said in a low, knowing, almost soothing voice. "Sit down, man. And listen."

He told me it had happened outside of Atlantic City in 2001. A mom, pushing her 4-year-old daughter in a stroller, had missed the

bus on 5th Street, and was running next to it so she could catch it at the stop on 6th. Mom tripped on a crack in the sidewalk, and the stroller shot out of her hands and went off the curb and under the bus.

Bus 8802 ground her up in the rear dual tires to the point that it took 4 hours to get all of her, and the stroller, out. The bus driver was so distraught that he killed himself later that night.

"So, *that's* who's on the bus? The little girl? Is *that* what you're tellin' me, man? Gimme a break—I don't believe in this ghost crap!" I yelled.

"Then maybe you'll believe this," Gussy said as he walked me over to a plaque on the wall. It was dedicated to J. Mackling, driver, died in 2001, member of the Consolidated Transit Drivers Union. Under the dedication was his picture. I stared at it.

"But … *that's* the guy I saw reading the book at the end of the washer, and in the bus," I said to Gussy.

"Yeah," Gussy whispered, sniffling back a tear. "Mack reads to her when she acts up and gets to bawlin' sometimes, you know."

***

I saw it tonight, drivin' down the pike, through the dark, lonely part of the Pines, out through Mullica Township, heading to Atlantic City. I could see the driver, slightly illuminated by the nightlights and gauges in the driver's compartment, but the rest of the bus was dark and looked like it was empty.

Empty, except for the two people I met, who will never get off at any of the stops 8802 makes.

I wonder what Mack is reading to the little girl tonight, as they roll, eternally together, through the Pine Barrens.

Jack in the Pulpit

Jack Morrison was a preacher who'd come to the Pine Barrens from Ireland in 1809. He was a fine man, and everybody around the little town of Chatsworth, where he finally settled, grew fond of him very quickly.

Before the first church was ever built in Chatsworth, Pastor Jack, as he came to be known, built a podium, or what he was fond of calling his pulpit, in a clearing near where he lived, next to an old cranberry bog, and preached his services there every Sunday morning. Since there was no bell to ring to summon his congregation, Pastor Jack would play his old harmonica, which echoed for miles around in the Pines, to call the townsfolk to service. Everybody in town showed up Sunday morning to hear Pastor Jack preach the gospel and to sing hymns together, as they stood around the pulpit in that small clearing.

Everybody, that is, but one man. And that man was Harry "the Hermit" Morton.

Now, there was something very peculiar about Harry the Hermit, which was his odor. The truth is, Harry *stunk*! He smelled so bad that nobody could stand to be near him and that's why he became a hermit. Folks around town would see Harry and run in the other direction. Why, there was even the story they used to tell in Chatsworth about the time Harry and several other local men were attacked by wild Indians, and how everybody was killed *except* Harry, because when the Indians smelled him, they thought the Spirit of the Dead lived in him and were afraid to kill him.

Well, by and by, these stories finally reached Pastor Jack, and, being the fine man of the Lord he was, he found himself feeling bad for Harry. Surely, there was something he could do for the poor old hermit. So, on a Tuesday afternoon in October, with the woods ablaze in their autumn colors, Pastor Jack went to the rundown old shack in the woods where Harry lived and knocked on the door. From inside, an angry voice growled, "Who goes there?"

"It is I, Pastor Jack Morrison, Harry," said Jack.

"What do you want?" Harry asked.

"I've come to invite you to services this Sunday. Please, Harry," Jack pleaded, "won't you come and worship with us?"

There was a long silence before Harry finally said, "I'll come to your service, but only if you can prove to me that you're in special standing with The Almighty, boy!"

Jack smiled, pleased that he seemed to be making progress with the bitter old man. "And just how do you suggest I do that, Harry?" he asked.

"Before you get to preachin' Sunday, I want you to walk across ol' Mr. White's cranberry bog, from one end to the other," snickered Harry. "If ya be special with the Lord, the way you oughta be, he'll save ya from sinkin'."

"OK, Harry, I'll do it," Jack called through the door of Harry's shack. "But then you'll have to promise me that you'll come to Sunday services each and every week from now on."

Harry said, "You'll do it, will ya? OK, then, you've got a deal, boy. Now, go away!"

Jack smiled the whole way as he walked back to town. He knew that old Mr. White's bog had been abandoned for years and was now just a flat, useless, sand-covered acre of ground that nobody bothered with. Jack was pleased that now, finally, he might be able to help poor, lonely old Harry the Hermit.

News that Harry had accepted Pastor Jack's invitation got around Chatsworth pretty quickly, and soon everyone in town was talking about it. And sure enough, on the following Sunday morning, when Jack called his congregation to service with his harmonica, the last one to show up was Harry.

As Harry approached the crowd, everyone except Pastor Jack could be seen lowering their heads and covering their noses with their hands, so bad was Harry's smell. Suddenly, Harry spoke.

"Ain't there somethin' you gotta do, boy?" Harry said to Jack.

"Yes, there is, Harry, true to me word!" Jack answered.

And, as Harry the Hermit Morton and the rest of the congregation looked on, Pastor Jack Morrison walked from his pulpit, across the clearing, and out onto old Mr. White's cranberry bog where he promptly sank from sight.

"Old bogs'll get 'em every time," was the last thing Harry the Hermit was heard to say as he walked back into the woods that day.

Well, no one ever saw old Pastor Jack Morrison *or* old Harry again. But, to this day, every spring, when the warm rains fall around the bogs and swamps in the Pine Barrens, you'll see a very peculiar and beautiful plant that begins to grow as the ground thaws.

And it's called a "Jack-in-the-Pulpit."

The Blood-Stained Waters of the Pine Barrens

For as long as anyone can remember, the water flowing in the streams and rivers of the Pine Barrens has been stained a peculiar, deep shade of red. Some folks call it "cedar water" and say that it has taken on the color of the vast stands of cedar trees that grow throughout the region. Others say that bog iron deposits give the water its unusual color. But legend tells a different story … about an Indian chief and the curse he put upon the once-clear waters that caused them to be forever stained with the blood of his people.

Early in the 1600s, an English ship full of new settlers slowly made its way up the Mullica River. It was right around Christmastime, and the settlers wanted to get ashore as quickly as they could because it was very cold, and the river was starting to freeze over. They hoped to get a settlement built in time to properly celebrate Christmas in their new land.

About 10 miles upriver, the ship became mired in sand and muck during a very low full moon tide. Try as they might, the men couldn't free the ship. The captain, a man named William Crowley, decided that everyone would have to leave the ship and wade or swim to shore, which they could see in the near distance. The passengers and crew made it safely to shore, but they were wet, hungry, and very, very cold.

Because food, water, and supplies would have been difficult if not impossible to bring ashore, there was nothing to eat and no tools that might have been used to build shelters. A few of the men had managed to bring their rifles and pistols, but little else. The settlers were very rightly concerned that they might freeze to death by morning.

Two young Indian children from the Lenni-Lenape tribe that lived in the area had been watching from the woods. Running back to their village, they told their story to their parents, who brought them before the chief, a man called Shamong. After hearing of the trouble the settlers were in, Chief Shamong called his tribe together and told them to gather some dried meat, corn, and warm blankets, along with some tools. They would take these things to the settlers and save them from freezing to death in the bitter cold Pine Barrens night.

In short time, the tribe had gathered the items and began their trek through the woods toward the place on the riverbank where the settlers were stranded. Back at the settlers' camp, someone saw the Indians coming and started screaming, "Indians! Indians!" The settlers panicked, believing they were about to be attacked and killed by savages.

The settlers who had managed to bring their firearms from the ship started shooting at the Indians. One by one, the Indians fell, mortally wounded, in the sand near the bank of the river. The last Indian to be shot was Chief Shamong, as he tried in vain to tell the settlers his people had come to help them. As he lay dying on the ground, Shamong was angry and deeply saddened that his people had died at the hands of these settlers whose lives they'd tried to save.

Finally, after discovering the provisions the Indians had been carrying, the settlers realized the tribe had been trying to help them and began treating the wounded. It was too little too late. Just before Chief Shamong died, he looked into the heavens and said, "May the blood that runs from my people into the sands and into the river forever stain these waters, so that what happened here is never forgotten."

To this day, Shamong's curse holds true and should serve to remind us to always think before we act, for the waters that run through the Pine Barrens are, now and forever, stained red with the blood of haste.

Cedar Water Blues

That ol' wading river runs down thru the pines,
Cuts thru Hawkins Bridge, y'all, runs past Point Divine.
Her red cedar waters caress Bodine's Field;
As she winds her way into the bay, I touch her and feel.

She's just like a woman, so fragile, yet strong,
She might bend a little, but won't stay too long.
Sometimes she gives life, sometimes takes it away.
She'll laugh as she buries what she killed, somewhere in the bay.

Keep flowin' my red lady, please don't become dammed.
Wash me on downstream, come, take my hand.
Take me on home, girl, make me one with your flood.
If I choose to drown, just take me down,
make me one with your blood.

Cedar water blues … Cedar water blues …

Dr. Mason's Patient

Other than the occasional songwriter, poet, or lollygagger who needs it to happen before they can get something done, nobody really thinks twice about a blue moon these days. But back in the mid-1800s, the folks who lived in a small Pine Barrens village called Bulltown had a good reason to celebrate the relatively rare astronomical occurrence. A blue moon is the second full moon in a given month, and the blue moon of October 1858 changed the lives of Bulltown residents by freeing them from the tyranny of a very strange man—a man whose demise was "memorialized by proxy," you might say, on one of the most recognizable products ever to come out of the Pines.

The man, of course, was the one and only Raymus O'Dell.

Nobody knew exactly where Raymus was from, to tell you the truth, or why he turned up in Bulltown. There were those who said he was an escaped slave from Georgia who had made his way north to the Jersey Pine Barrens. Others said he was a nationalized English deckhand, originally from the Congo, who had jumped ship in Philadelphia, having arrived, coincidentally, right after the "Devil's Footprints" were discovered in Devon, England. Still others claimed (usually after several swigs from the apple oil jug) that he just appeared one evening in front of Green's General Store on Bulltown Road—the main street through town—with that mule, cart, and harmonica of his, and started his carryin'-ons that wound up terrorizing Bulltown's folk and ended up with Raymus at the end of a long hank of 2-inch-thick braided hemp rope.

Raymus O'Dell was damned peculiar right from the start, when he first appeared. To begin with, he'd only show up in town on the evening of a full moon, just before it got dark. Then there was his appearance. He carried a cane and wore a black tuxedo with tails, a bright yellow shirt with red, frilly ruffles on each side of the buttons, and a top hat. A very large red feather rose from just above the brim of his hat, fastened with a silver band.

Peculiar, too, was the ice-blue color of Raymus's eyes. They were cold and intense—"scary-cold" in the words of the townsfolk—and particularly striking set against the blackest skin anyone in Bulltown had ever seen. Those eyes insisted on your complete attention, and, once they got it, it was hard to break away.

But perhaps the *most* peculiar thing about Raymus is what he'd say and do after jumping down off his wagon each month when he came into town. He'd spring from his seat, hit the ground, smile, and say, "I'm the only patient Dr. Mason didn't kill, so pay me now or pay me later, but pay me, yes, you will!"

Then Raymus would start stomping his right foot in the dirt to set and keep time, and he'd play a strange, eerily haunting tune on his harmonica. The music seemed to hang in its own echo, settling over the Pine Barrens like wet mist. "Music that were wet with sin" is what most folks said who heard it.

As if a powerful, unseen magnet was somehow switched on, when Raymus started playing, folks in earshot dropped whatever they were doing to gather around him. They'd just stand there, listening. They didn't sing. They didn't hum along or tap their feet or dance. They'd just listen, looking into the strange, ice-blue eyes of this strange man nobody really knew a thing about.

After Raymus finished playing his harp, he'd tuck it in a pocket on the inside of his coat, smile, flip his top hat off his head, and shake it slightly at the end of his outstretched arm. "Pay me now, or pay me later, but pay me, yes, you will!" he'd say over and over again. And even though these were lean times in Bulltown, somehow, each month, Raymus managed to threaten his way to a good many coins going into that hat. It was as though folks were afraid to see what would happen if they *didn't* pay Raymus.

Jed and Jane Hoffman and their family were the first to find out.

It was January 1858. The nonsense with Raymus, as most people thought of it, was in its third year. Folks had been very generous on December's full moon with Raymus's hand-out because of Christmas and all, but it was an extraordinarily cold and snowy winter taking place, and it looked like it was going to continue. Everything in the Pines was frozen and caked with ice and snow, making life that much harder. It was so cold that the coal buggers—men who made charcoal for a living—were finding it extremely difficult to cut enough wood to feed the glasshouse furnaces in Bulltown, Crowleytown, and Green Bank. Men were getting frostbite, saws and axes were "sticking" in the cold, and life and income money were slowing down like molasses.

Jed Hoffman was a coal bugger with 12 years of experience under his belt. His hands were frost-nipped and hurt like the devil with "the rheumatoid" from using them every day of his life to try to earn a living. When Raymus came to town on that cold January evening, Jed stood there listening to him, along with his wife and several other families who were in town doing chores, just long enough for Raymus to get about one minute into his song.

Suddenly, Jed raised his hands up in the air and hollered, "You can stop right there, 'cause I ain't payin'!"

A deafening quiet filled the air as Raymus stood there, seemingly staring straight through Jed with his cold blue eyes, then finally saying, "I'm the only patient Dr. Mason didn't kill, so pay me now or pay me later, but pay me, yes, you will!"

"No, I won't!" Jed said loudly. "I don't give a damn *whose* patient you are or ever were. I don't give a damn what's wrong with you, who you are, or where you're from. I work way too hard for my money, and I ain't giving it to *you*! I need every penny for me and mine this month! Let's go, Jane!"

And with that, Jed and Jane turned and headed down the street toward their home without paying Raymus or even bothering to look back. They hadn't walked more than a hundred yards when the telltale column of black smoke started rising up into the deepening purple of the cold dusk sky.

"It's the Hoffman place!" someone in the crowd yelled. Jed and Jane were running toward their home now, and as folks in the crowd started to follow, Raymus called out, "I'm the only patient Dr. Mason didn't kill, so pay me now or pay me later, but pay me, yes, you will!"

They all turned, except the Hoffmans, and dropped coins into Raymus's hat as he stood there smiling a big smile, then continued as a group toward the Hoffman place to try to help put out the fire.

It was too late. The house had burnt to the ground. The many neighbors who had come to help just stood there in disbelief. The Hoffmans hadn't paid Raymus, and now their home was in ashes. Raymus's warnings, went the whispers in the crowd, were to be taken seriously, and in fact, they were from that night forward. On the rare occasion when they weren't, or couldn't be heeded, folks suffered the consequences.

In March, Dan Milnes happened to hear Raymus playing but had spent all his money earlier on some blacksmithing tools. Returning home that evening, he found all four of his horses dead.

In April, the Zane farm burnt down after Charlie Zane dropped a fake coin into Raymus's hat.

In May, none of the Fergusons' asparagus crop grew after Chet Ferguson tried to play along with Raymus on his fiddle, refusing to pay Raymus because, as he told the crowd, "Well, he ain't gonna pay *me*!"

And so it went for the rest of that summer in Bulltown. Raymus came to town each full moon and played, and if anyone heard it and didn't pay, catastrophe would follow.

After Raymus's visit in September, word of a secret meeting, to be held at Green's General Store, got around town. Most of the men in the area showed up for it. It was Jed Hoffman who spoke first.

"As you-ins might or may not know, there's a blue moon comin' in October, and I'll be damned if I'm gonna pay that nasty old sum'bitch twighst in one month. I vote we grab and hang him! As soon as he pulls up in that wagon, we gang-rush him, poke out those starin'-blue eyes so he can't trance anybody to death with 'em, and string him up right and proper out front here in that buttonwood tree." The vote was unanimous. Hang Raymus!

And so, on the evening of the blue moon in October 1858, Raymus O'Dell pulled into town, jumped down from his wagon, pulled out his harmonica, stomped his foot in the dirt, and started playing that eerie song. After a few seconds, he stopped abruptly. He was playing to nobody! Not a soul was to be seen, as if the town had been deserted. Raymus looked around and around, again and again, then suddenly shouted, "I'm the only patient Dr. Mason didn't kill, so pay me now or pay me later, but pay me, yes, you will!"

Suddenly, the saloon started smoking. Then Green's General Store burst into flames, followed by some of the smaller shops and houses on the street. It seemed that smoke was rising from every building in Bulltown, as if the entire town was burning.

All at once, from behind Green's, some 50 men rushed out into the street and tackled Raymus to the ground, and as fast as you could shake the stick that was used to poke out those strange, scary-blue eyes, Raymus was hanging from the big old buttonwood tree in front of Green's. Jed grabbed Raymus's harp, threw it into the dirt, and stomped on it, breaking it into pieces. Then the men ran into the woods to escape the burning town, leaving Raymus behind. Even as he was dying on the end of a rope he was heard to say, "I'm the only patient Dr. Mason didn't kill, so pay me now or pay me later, but pay me, yes, you will!"

When the townsfolk returned in the morning, their town was gone—burned completely to the ground, save for the buttonwood tree they'd hanged Raymus from. Under the tree, a small pile of ashes was all that was left of Raymus.

Since then, and to this day, buttonwood doesn't burn very well. Some say it was the curse Raymus put on that tree, and all buttonwoods, just before he died that caused the demise of the charcoal industry in the Pines.

It was Jane Hoffman who scooped up Raymus's ashes, putting them in a jar so he could later be buried, being the good Christian soul that she was. On a piece of paper she glued to the jar with pine sap, she wrote, "RAYMUS O'DELL ? 1858." But when her husband Jed saw it, he said in anger, "We aren't ever going to hear, mention, or write that man's name again around here, as far as I'm concerned!" He scratched out what Jane had written, and instead wrote: "MASON'S PATIENT (WITHOUT THE EYES) ? 1858."

Jed, who'd found work as a wooden mold maker at the Crowleytown Glass Works near Bulltown, kept that jar full of Raymus's ashes on top of his whittling tool chest. He looked at it several times a day for years and years while he was carving the wooden molds used by the glassblowers, thankful that the reign of the man contained therein was cut short and proud that he had been instrumental in bringing it about.

One morning, whilst having his coffee, an idea, along with a smile, came to Jed after he looked at Raymus's jar of ashes with the note that he and Jane had written still stuck to it.

It took close to a week, but he carved a solid maple fruit jar mold that would go on to be used to make thousands and thousands of fruit jars, recognizable the world over. The jar would become synonymous with the Pine Barrens and set Crowleytown Glass Works firmly in history's glasshouse hall of fame. It also served as a kind of secret commemorative item among those who remembered what happened in Bulltown in the fall of 1858.

To this very day, you can find Jed's jars in use and proudly displayed in antique shops and on collectors' shelves all over the world, bearing the words: MASON'S PATENT 1858.

So you see, Jed Hoffman made sure with that stick on Bulltown Road, and later with his wood mold carving tools, that to this day Mason's "patient" has no eyes.

The Ballad of Raymus O'Dell

I wanna tell you a story
'Bout a man that we buried,
His name was Raymus O'Dell.
He'd come to town every month
When the moon would shine full,
We swore that Raymus was the Devil Himself.
He'd stop at the store, tie up his mule and his wagon,
Then tip his hat with a smile.
He'd take a harp from his shirt,
Stomp his foot in the dirt,
And then he'd play an evil song in the night.

When Raymus finished his playin'
We would throw him a gold coin,
And "pay the devil His due,"
'Cause if you heard what he played and didn't bother to pay,
The story went he'd come a-callin' on you.
He'd burn your barn and he'd kill all your horses,
Your crops would fail, then you'd die.
The whole town gathered around
Each month he came into town,
He'd take our money then ride off into the night.

A blue moon came in October 1858,
Now we'd be damned if we would pay Raymus twice.
So we voted to hang him out in front of the store,
Me and the posse waited for him that night.
We heard that harp play its song,
Then the saloon started burnin',
The rest was gone with the sun.
But though our town had burned down
We finally silenced his sound,
Once and for all when the hangin' was done.

He said not a word before that rope noose was tightened,
And just before Raymus died,
I took the harp from his shirt, and stomped it into the dirt,
It seemed the fittin' way to tell him goodbye.

Well, we built a new town with the help of the railroad,
And now, when the moon rises blue,
Nobody pays half a mind to that man we called Raymus,
Let alone pay him two.
Let alone pay him two.
Let alone pay him two.

The Whiter and Blacker Spikes

Long, long ago, back when New Jersey was still an English colony, there were only two roads that led travelers to and from the town of Camden. They weren't much more than footpaths until the stagecoaches started using them. That widened them a bit, but for the most part, they were still little more than dirt ruts that led, by and by, into the dense, foreboding, and still largely unexplored-by-white-men Pine Barrens.

Both roads started at exactly the same place back then, about a half-mile from the Camden-to-Philadelphia ferry-launching point on the Delaware River, quite near the site of today's Cooper Hospital. To keep travelers and the stagecoach drivers sure of which road was which, a large white spike was hammered into the ground on the left side of the road, and a large black spike was hammered into the right side of the road. Depending on your desired destination, you either started out at and kept to the side of the road nearer the whiter spike or the blacker spike, until they clearly split and went in their own directions. The road of the whiter spike headed easterly, and the road of the blacker spike headed more southeasterly. Strangely enough, both roads started at the same place in Camden, and both roads ended in the same place, some 60 miles away, out on Absecon Island in the Atlantic Ocean. That place would later be called Atlantic City.

Travelers started calling the roads by the color of the spike from whence they started: the Whiter Spike or the Blacker Spike. They simply dropped the word "road" altogether. These were the two main routes through South Jersey in those days, and many a story came back from the travelers and stagecoach drivers who wound their ways over them, to and from God-knows-where.

One such story involved a stagecoach driver by the name of Collings Wood. Collings followed the whiter spike side of the road on his trips, heading true east, and became very fond of the gal who owned a tavern where he'd stop the stagecoach for his luncheon. The gal's name was Nella Warwick. There was a sign in front of the tavern that read: "STOP AND SAY HI, NELLA!" Before too long, the place became known simply as "Hi-Nella's."

Nella was a robust, bawdy kind of woman given to practical jokes and downright trickery. Many folks said it was the effects of too much drinking, and still others said she was just crazy. It mattered little to Collings. All he knew was that he liked her … a lot.

One day while having his lunch, Collings told Nella how fond he was of her. Nella told him that in order to prove how fond he truly was of her, she would require him to bring her the now-famous whiter spike from the beginning of the road in Camden. "And," she said, "I will require you to pitch that spike from your moving stagecoach, and into the roof of my tavern, allowing me to use it as a lightning rod, a landmark, or whatever else I may see fit for its use!"

Sure enough, the next time Collings approached Nella's tavern, he reached back to the top of the stagecoach and grabbed the famous whiter spike that he'd pulled from the beginning of the road

in Camden earlier that morning. As he approached Hi-Nella's, he pitched the spike with all his might, sending it flying toward the tavern. Unfortunately, as Nella stood on the porch of the tavern, watching the goings-on that were happening in front of her, the spike fell short of the intended roof and ran straight through her chest, killing her instantly.

To this day, anyone born and raised in South Jersey, when asked, will tell you that the whiter spike *still* runs straight through Hi-Nella.

Another "spike" story involves the first example of that truly American pastime: rum-runnin'. Only in this case, it wasn't rum or moonshine, but a drink made from fermented honey called mead. Down-Jersey Pine Barrens mead was fast becoming the preferred libation in the upper-crust circles of Philadelphia's "high society." Benjamin Franklin himself was said to be a great admirer, and copious consumer, of South Jersey Pine Barrens mead.

Sneaking (or "runnin'" as it was called back then) the mead from South Jersey across the Delaware on the ferry and into Philadelphia could bring great monetary reward for those daring but foolhardy enough to try such an undertaking. In those days, bringing alcohol from one colony into another was forbidden by the king and the governors of the colonies, and if caught, a "runner" could face a lengthy stint in jail or in the public stocks, or worse. But the market was such as to justify the action by daring and skilled "runners"—men (and the occasional woman) who would sneak, on horseback, through the extremely dense hardwood stands and swamps that made up the Big Timber Creek region where the mead was made and jugged, and needed only to be carried to waiting consumers.

Many a poor man trying to put food on the table, after much thought, told his wife and closest friends, "Well, I guess I'm gonna get to runnin' mead across the blacker spike." This region was traversed by the blacker spike road.

It's widely agreed to this day that the Black Horse Pike is always the best road to take when a man needs to get to runnin' mead—or to "Runnemede," as the place where it all went down is called today.

The Goin's-Ons Out on Purgatory Road

There's no tellin' and, for that matter, no reasonin' for the goin's-ons that have been goin' on out on Purgatory Road all these years. Years that stretch back for longer than most anyone can remember.

Purgatory Road runs off of Eayrestown Road, just north of Red Lion, out there on the fringes of the Pine Barrens in Burlington County. And it's at that intersection of Eayrestown and Purgatory roads that one of the strangest and most mysterious goin's-ons still goes on. I'm talking about the old lady and her cart.

Nobody knows who she is or where she comes from, or even where she goes, but one thing is for sure: When she gets to callin' for "Willie, Billy, Silly-Jillie and Millie" over and over again, and the way she turns to the North, East, South, and then West when she's doin' her callin,' it will send the goomblies and gumblies straight up your back, and have you hunting for the rabbit that's runnin' over your grave!

There's another thing for sure. When that old telephone rings in her cart and she picks up the receiver and says, "Willie, Billy, Silly-Jillie, Millie! Is that *you*?" you'll think *you're* losin' *your* mind. How that phone rings is anybody's guess, and who she talks to on the other end of that receiver is still any other anybody's guess. It's a very strange set of goin's-ons is all anybody really knows for sure. And like I said, it's *still* goin' on. You just have to be there at the right time, which is any time, according to the folks who have seen and heard the old lady with the cart.

Some folks say her name is Dolores and that the names she calls belong to her husband and kids who perished in the house fire that happened out there on Purgatory Road in the 1950s. It's believed that her son, Billy, started the fire one night whilst trying to make gunpowder in the cellar, that Dolores was the only one to get out of the place alive, and that the grief sent her stark-raving mad. She was never able to accept her terrible loss, and now she roams the area, day in and day out, looking for and calling for her beloved family—for 60 years and better now. The thing is, she still looks the same today as when her searchin' first started back in 1957. She doesn't age. She doesn't get a new cart or a new phone. She just calls and calls and calls to her family, and answers the phone once in awhile when it rings.

Then there's the matter of Mr. Stare-itis. He pulls up to the same house on Purgatory Road every day at 5:17 PM, stops his car, and stares. Who knows who or what he stares at, or why, but that's what he does. Every day, like clockwork, Monday through Friday, rain or shine, snow or sleet, or thunderstorm or perfect calm.

For years now, the few neighbors in the area have called the cops on Mr. Stare-itis when they see him pull up and stare at that house. The State Police are right down Route 206, not two miles away at the Red Lion Barracks. But they never get to Purgatory Road in time. Folks have written down the license plate number and given it to the cops when they *do* arrive. But the cops say the same thing every time: That plate doesn't exist, and it never did.

Curly black hair with a thin mustache and cold, cold blue eyes is how folks describe Mr. Stare-itis. Intense-looking. Almost sad. Never says a word. He just stares. And stares. And stares. At that house, out there on Purgatory Road.

Then there was the incident at the Peschko home, out there on Purgatory Road.

Mrs. Peschko had gone to fetch her husband at work in Chatsworth, after he'd called to report that his car had broken down. She left her 9-year-old son to look after the baby, her 1-year-old daughter, and instructed him not to leave the house.

Some time had passed after she left, when, all of a sudden, the boy heard footsteps falling heavily and coming up the stairs from the cellar. He quickly ran to the cellar door and locked it. There was someone screaming and shouting—a man, he later said—on the other side of that door, demanding to be let out and threatening to kill him in a horrid voice and language.

The boy picked up his baby sister, made a beeline for the front door, and ran out into the front yard, where he sat with his sister and cried until his parents arrived some time later.

The boy, barely able to speak, recounted the events to his parents, at which time his father became extremely angry and admonished him for making up "tall stories." He was sent to bed without dinner and cried himself asleep.

The next morning, his mother was waiting for him at the breakfast table, having prepared his favorite breakfast of scrapple and eggs. She spoke in a calm, restorative, and assuring voice.

"After you went to bed last night, your father unlocked the cellar door and went into the cellar. He found everything down there broken and ripped to shreds. Every box was upset. Slats in the coal bin were broken in half like splinters. Christmas ornaments and tinsel was thrown around. But that's all he found. No one was down there. None of the windows were broken, and remain nailed shut, even now. We called the police and they came but were unable to find anything. Now, eat your scrapple and eggs and don't give this incident any more thought. Everything's OK."

Yep, there's no tellin' and, for that matter, no reasonin' for the goin's-ons that have been goin' on, and *keep* goin' on, out on Purgatory Road all these years. Years that stretch back for longer than most anyone can remember. Perhaps the road itself remembers, recalling and replaying events that took place on it over and over again. Events that are locked in Purgatory … forever.

Birth of the Tides and Seasons

For centuries, scientists and astronomers have been telling us that the ocean's tides are caused by the moon's gravitational pull on the Earth. They tell us that the up and down motion of the world's oceans, pulled and pushed by these gravitational forces, is what causes the Earth to wobble on its axis, and that this wobbling is the cause of the changing of the seasons.

Though it is true that the Earth's wobbling on its axis is responsible for the changing seasons, the *real* reason for the ocean's tides has nothing to do with the moon. The tides were born, along with the changing of the seasons, one day very long ago at the edge of the Pine Barrens, in the body of water that today we call the Great Egg Harbor Bay. And here's what *really* happened that started the restlessness of the world's oceans, and the changing of the four seasons that continues to this day.

Long, long before the white man came to America, an annual event took place (and continued for some time after Europeans arrived) on the shores of the Great Egg Harbor Bay. Millions of seagulls would lay their eggs on the miles and miles of beaches that surround this body of water. Tens of millions of eggs would lie there, waiting to hatch into chicks, which is how the Great Egg Harbor Bay was named by Swedish settlers in the mid-17th century.

The Native People all over the eastern part of North America would wait for and plan their lives around this annual event, so important was it for supplying a large portion of their food during the year. They would arrive in the Pine Barrens by the tens of thousands to gather the eggs, putting aside any tribal differences or hostilities they might have had with each other during the year, and co-existing peacefully for the yearly gathering of the eggs, which they called *absegominicon* (AB-sa-GO-ma-NIK-in).

The eggs provided high-quality protein and were eaten raw or cooked in any number of ways. They could be preserved by being buried in the cool earth or mixed with other grains and foods. Even without being preserved, they lasted a long time, as there were no extreme changes in the weather back then, just one continuous cool season.

What's more, the eggshells were found to improve bone strength when ground into a fine powder and added to food. This shell powder was given to other egg-laying birds the Native People raised, as it strengthened their shells and was used as a coloring agent in inks and paints. In short, these seagull eggs were very important to the survival of the Native People, and the annual gathering along the shores of the Great Egg Harbor Bay was a major event in their lives.

While the Native People gathered millions of eggs during *absegominicon*, they were always careful to leave a sufficient number on the beaches to hatch and continue the species, ensuring that future generations would benefit from this key food source. One year, however, as the thousands of Native People were arriving, a huge, powerful whirlwind blew into the Pine Barrens just after the seagulls had finished laying. As the eggs were blown into the bay, each and every one sank beneath the surface of the water.

The Native People, having to hold onto trees or dig their fingers into the ground to keep from being blown into the water themselves, were horrified and panicked as they watched the eggs sink out of sight. Not only would they be deprived of a vital part of their yearly nourishment, but this might also spell the ultimate demise of the seagull population, as *every* egg that had been laid was gone!

When the wind subsided, the Native People settled down a bit and gathered in large groups, caring and tending to those who had been scraped up or otherwise hurt during the storm. A chief named Tuckaho, from the local tribe of Lenni-Lenape, gathered his people around him and said, "So many of the People will become sick from hunger, and perhaps even starve to death if we cannot gather the eggs this year. And we will lose the gulls forever. We must find a way to rescue the eggs from the water!"

Tuckaho thought and thought, and eventually went into a trance as he looked out over the Great Egg Harbor Bay. In his trance state, he recalled playing as a child in a small pool of water, and how he and some friends would stand in the middle of the pool and raise themselves up and down, doing deep knee bends in unison, causing a large swell of water to gather in the middle, and a large wave to wash over the edges. If he could create such a wave in the middle of the Great Egg Harbor Bay, it would push the eggs back up onto the beaches, and they could be gathered.

He awoke from his trance, and yelled loudly, "The 'Great One' has given me the answer!"

Tuckaho stood on a stump of a tree that had blown over in the great wind and, cupping his hands so that all could hear, he told the People of his plan. They were to gather in the middle of the Great Egg Harbor Bay (it being only 4 feet at its deepest back then), and, on his cue, slowly start bending at the knees in a coordinated up and down motion, creating waves that would push the eggs back onto the beaches where they could be collected and *absegominicon*, along with the next generation of gulls, would be saved.

As the Native People listened, a cheer rose up unlike anything ever heard before. It seemed that, indeed, Tuckaho's plan would work!

At Tuckaho's signal, all of the People ran into the bay and gathered in the middle, not realizing they had just trampled on and broken most of the eggs. Tuckaho, in the middle of the gathered crowd, started yelling, "Up … down … up … down …"

The People followed his cue, and soon great waves began forming and emanating out in every direction, some toward the shore to the west, and some out into the ocean to the east. So great were these waves, that they did finally reach the shoreline and push the few remaining untrampled eggs onto the beach, saving the seagull population, since these eggs did finally hatch later. But as the waves washed back into the bay, they swelled over the heads of the People who were creating them, drowning most of them before joining the waves that had pushed into the sea, strengthening them, and doubling and tripling them in size.

The waves spread out all across the ocean and caused a great weight redistribution in and disruption *on* the once perfectly balanced, calm, and placid surface. This, in turn, started the world wobbling as it tried to rebalance itself, thus tilting it on its axis and causing the changing of the seasons. As it wobbled more and more, the weight of the water against the axis caused a gyro-like reaction that, in turn, disrupted the world's *other* oceans, turning them all into the wave-wrought bodies of water we know today.

Thus, the raising and flattening of water on the Earth's surface, called *tides*, and the changing of the seasons, which is due to the tilt and wobble of the Earth on its axis, were set in motion centuries ago by a few thousand Native Americans in the Pine Barrens, as they tried to save their food supply.

This remarkable incident explains why, to this day, the gulls can't help laughing at us.

The Legend of Big-Eared Challie

For as long as anyone can remember, even the folks who wrote books and told stories a hundred years ago, Challie—aka Charles Wills—has been settin' by himself in the same place in the Pine Barrens, just off Eagle Road between Friendship and Chatsworth.

It's a nice, quiet spot, with a railin' for leanin' if you want, which is befittin' o' Challie, 'cause that's the special thing *about* Challie: He's nice … and quiet.

Challie has the biggest ears, which makes him the best listener you'll ever meet in your life, I assure you, because he never says a word. But he listens so intently to whatever problem or mystery or question you might bring him that it somehow seems to work itself out before it's time to leave. And that's why so many people, down through the years, have come to know and call Challie by that name: "Big-Eared Challie." He's all ears. No pie hole!

Folks with their problems, mysteries, and questions have been "givin' it up to Challie" or "takin' it to Challie" darn near forever, it seems. In fact, havin' Challie help solve one's problems became so popular in the 1860s that members of the Union Army, who were just leaving a "talkin' to" with Challie about their fears of their demise, overheard some Rebs talkin' to him about their fears of the "secret fight" comin' up in a place in Pennsylvania called Gettysburg. One of the Union soldiers, Theodore Eaves, wrote what he heard on some paper and dropped it in a messenger's pouch that made its way to General Meade and the Union Army powers-that-be, and, well, the rest is history. The word "eavesdropping" found its way into the English language because of Challie, and I guess it's safe to say that Ol' Chal helped decide the outcome of the Civil War.

Challie has even helped create some world-renowned art. While visiting southern New Jersey in 1850, noted poet and writer Walt Whitman journeyed into the Pine Barrens after hearing about and wanting to meet this "Challie fellow" for himself.

Walt reportedly found and spent several days with Challie, talking with him, contemplating and taking in all that was said and writing in his tablets as he leaned on Challie's railing. Whitman was said to have been "utterly perplexed" that fallen pine needles, and not leaves, made up and nourished the soils in the Barrens. Five years later, he published "Leaves of Grass," and there are those who say that "O Captain! My Captain!" was originally called "Challie! Yo Challie!"—the proof being in the third verse, as Whitman writes about lips that are pale and silent, or something along those lines.

Whitman was reportedly so thankful for the big ears Challie offered him that he dropped a coin in a small covered bucket that sat near Challie every time he wrote a line in his notebook. Upon returning to Camden after his sojourn into the Pine Barrens, Walt reportedly told friends, "I offered Challie a coin for every phrase I wrote in that book, such was my concentration on account of that man's aura and quiet." And that is where the saying "to coin a phrase" came from. Again, directly or indirectly, it's thanks to good ol' Challie!

In more recent times, the story goes that the late Don Hewitt, creator of the acclaimed CBS news program *60 Minutes*, found Challie one afternoon in 1967. Hewitt had retreated into the Pine Barrens, knowing of their peace and solitude, because he had to make a hard decision as to what theme song *60 Minutes* was going to use. There were many choices, composed by many friends and colleagues, and he simply couldn't decide. Happening by chance upon Challie as he walked through the Pines, Hewitt was so taken with the quiet and solitude as he stood with Challie in "the middle of nowhere," that all he could hear was the ticking of his watch. In a eureka moment, Hewitt reportedly clapped his hands once and shouted at Challie, "That's it!" To this day, there never has been any theme music for the show, just the ticking of a watch—thanks to the peace and quiet of the Pine Barrens … and to Challie!

Good ol' Big-Eared Challie! We've interacted many times, he and I. And I always come away a little happier and more at peace with myself after each interaction. I'm glad we met, and I'm glad he's there. He'll always be there, will Challie. Just like his Pine Barrens, where he will forever rest in peace.

The Secret of Salamander Pond

Growing up in South Jersey, I was never very far from the woods or, indeed, the Pine Barrens. My favorite pastime was exploring what my friends and I were sure were never-before-seen-by-the-white-man places within a day's walking distance of where we lived. Following old, abandoned railroad tracks and tracing creeks and streams to their sources made for long days of excitement and discovery. Learning to use a compass and a map in the Boy Scouts ensured I never got lost as we ventured deep into the forest and off the familiar pathways, though my friends and I actually *tried* to get lost several times.

On one of these excursions into the wilds, we discovered a place that became very special to us. It was a spring at the end of a small, winding creek we'd been following through the swamps and brambles. We named it Salamander Pond, and the four of us who found it that day—me, Donnie, Bobby, and Richard—made a promise never to reveal its true location for as long as we lived. To my knowledge, it's still our secret, and, as far as I'm concerned, it will remain so.

Salamander Pond was only 5 feet across and a few inches deep, yet it was a special place—and not just because it bound us together through its shared secrets, though it did that. The first thing that made the spring unique was that although it was way, *way* back in a nearly inaccessible part of the woods, someone—we figured maybe the Indians who had lived in the area in earlier centuries—had gone to a lot of trouble building a square-ish stone wall, about a foot high, surrounding three sides of the pond. You could see that the stones, mostly no more than baseball-sized, were well-worn and very old-looking. They had been meticulously placed, one on top of another, in a kind of squared-off horseshoe pattern that blocked three sides and let the water flow out into the stream. There were strange markings scratched on the stones that comprised the top layer, including arrows, squares, triangles, and broken circles with lines through them.

The water that flowed from Salamander Pond was crystal clear and ice cold, and appeared to be the only source of the little stream that had led us to it. We would all bend down on our knees and drink from it every time we visited the place. After we had our fill of water, we would sit around the spring in a circle and very carefully move the sand at the bottom with our fingers. Suddenly, and inevitably, a salamander—an amphibian that resembles a four-legged spotted worm, 2 or 3 inches long, with a tail—would try to dart away from our fingers as we tried to catch it.

We would try to catch these salamanders for hours, putting the ones we caught into a steel bucket we brought along for this purpose. Once we'd tired of this activity, we'd release the salamanders back into the spring so they'd be there for us the next time. And they always were, to the point that we started recognizing them by their spots and giving them names.

Until one day.

It was starting to get cool out. The summer was over, and we were all back in school. Our trips to Salamander Pond had become infrequent after-school or weekend affairs. Traipsing through the woods, we could see the leaves starting to turn and smell the swamps "working"—giving off that telltale sweet, musty-gassy smell of summer's green foliage as they began to decompose, adding yet another layer of history to the ancient, time-fertilized, quagmire earth.

After our customary sip of the ice-cold water, we began the finger fishing, as we'd come to call it, trying to disrupt and draw the salamanders from their hiding places beneath the sand and near the bottom of the rocks surrounding the spring. Nothing. Five, 10, 15, then 20 minutes went by, and there was not a salamander to be seen. Where had they all gone?

"Maybe they're hibernating," Donnie said. "Dig down a little deeper in the sand. Maybe it'll wake 'em up or something."

No sooner had Donnie finished his sentence, we heard a rustling sound from deep in the woods. It sounded as though someone, unseen as yet, was taking a few quick steps, then stopping, taking a few quick steps more, then stopping again. As suddenly as the sound had begun, it stopped. We were all sitting around the spring, motionless, listening intently as the woods grew completely silent. I slowly stood up and scoped the area in all directions, peering into the woods, and even up into the branches, but I saw nothing.

"Maybe it was a deer," I said to my friends as I bent down and dug my hands deep into the sandy bottom of Salamander Pond. Scooping out two cupped handfuls of sand, I laid it off to the side of the wall, then stuck my hands back in for more, waiting for the water to clear before cupping more sand.

The next thing that happened changed my life forever in many, many ways. As I pushed my hands deep into the sand, the sound of someone whistling the strangest, spookiest melody imaginable came drifting to us on the wind. The tone was flute-like, but it was definitely a person out in the woods whistling, and it appeared to be directed right at us.

We all stood up and peered through the woods in the direction of the whistling. We could see nothing, but we could still hear that spooky, lilting sound. It was so strange and scary-sounding that it raised the hairs on our arms, and I began to feel sick to my stomach.

"What the *hell* is *that*?" I whispered to my friends, looking around in all directions, still seeing no one but my buddies.

"I'm going home now," Richard said, his eyes wide and tearing up with fear. His lips were quivering as he picked up his empty salamander bucket. "I got homework!"

"Me, too!" the rest of us said together in one voice.

As we started heading out of the woods, we looked around to see who was watching us, whistling that strange, haunting tune. A few steps away from the spring, I stopped and yelled, "Wait!" I ran back to the spring and pushed the mound of sand I had scooped up earlier back into the water with my foot, wanting to leave things as I'd found them—a concept I'd learned from both the Boy Scouts and the YMCA Indian Guides. As the sand fell in, I saw a perfectly round, flat little stone, about the size of a silver dollar, dropping into the water with it. I must have scooped it out of the spring with the sand, but I hadn't seen or felt it when I'd laid the sand next to the wall. I picked it up and looked at it as I hurried back to my friends.

"Look at this!" I said, excitedly. "It's a perfectly round stone that was in the sand I scooped out of the pond!"

Suddenly, the whistling stopped. We turned around in unison, trying to catch a glimpse of the person we knew must be out there, watching us, but silence now filled the air. We stood there for a minute, looking, listening. Nothing.

Then we heard the rustling sound again, from somewhere in the woods. It began softly but quickly grew louder as someone drew closer. The four of us exchanged horrified glances before nearly running over each other trying to be the first to get out of the woods and away from our unknown pursuer.

We were running so hard, and tripping over one another so often, that we actually started laughing, probably trying to disguise our intense fear, and screaming, "Get the hell out of the way!" as we looked back to see if anyone was following us.

By the time we reached the road at the edge of the woods, we were covered head to foot with swamp muck and bleeding scratches from the sticker bushes we'd run through. Walking up the road, heading home, we were continually looking behind us as we discussed what had happened and wondered who in the world could have been back there, watching us, whistling, then chasing us.

It was a bona-fide mystery, and we loved it now that we were safely walking up a paved road, out of the fright-spawning thickness and darkness of the woods. What had been four petrified-with-fright kids a few minutes ago were now four brave explorers, laughing and punching and pushing each other as if nothing had happened. We had prevailed and somehow emerged victorious over some unknown, unseen, lurking evil, even if we did keep checking over our shoulders to see what or who was following us.

"Hey!" Bobby said to me. "Where's that cool stone you found in the pond?"

I reached into my pants pocket and pulled out the stone. We stopped walking as everyone took their turn and looked at it, handled it, smelled it, rubbed it, and otherwise monkeyed around with it.

"Man alive, this thing is really heavy! But it feels and looks like sandstone, doesn't it?" Donnie said as he tossed and flipped it up and down in his hand, almost dropping it.

"Gimme it back, man!" I said to him as we started walking up the road again.

"What do *you* think it is?" he asked as he handed it back to me.

"It's a stone, duh!" I said, throwing it up in the air and out in front of us in a high arc.

The stone landed in the street and smashed into pieces when it hit the hard pavement, revealing a shiny golden coin that went rolling up the street. "Oh, man!" we all said together. We ran up to it, and it was the shiniest thing any of us had ever seen! The coin had somehow become encrusted in the stone-like stuff that had shattered off when it hit the pavement.

I bent down and picked it up.

"*Maannn*! *Cooool*!" we all said. Each of us again took turns touching it and smelling it and tossing it up and down as we stood there in the street. It had strange letters and numbers on one side, some of them resembling the markings on the top layer of rocks back at Salamander Pond. On the other side was a strange-looking, block-ended cross in a circle. Other strange letters and numbers surrounded the cross.

None of us knew what it was or how much it might be worth as we stood there, asking these questions amongst ourselves. Maybe it was the lost loot of Prohibition-era gangster robbers. Maybe it was from the days of the pirates who had once roamed South Jersey, according to the stories we'd heard. Maybe it was from the Romans.

"The *Romans*!" I said to Bobby. "Man, are you nuts? There weren't no Romans around here! The Romans lived in *Africa*!"

We laughed all the way home, hemming and hawing as we tried to guess what this object was that had come out of a rock from Salamander Pond. We agreed not to say anything to our parents because we figured if *they* didn't take it and keep it for themselves, they'd probably make us turn it in to someone, and we'd lose it.

Looking back, that was the last time for quite awhile that we would laugh and cut up and be carefree kids together.

Grabbing the coin out of Richard's hand, I put it in my pocket and said, "We gotta go back there on Saturday and dig some more, you guys. There might be a lot more of these in the pond. Hell, there might be tons of 'em scattered all down that stream, too!"

We all agreed to go again on Saturday. We also promised and shook hands on it walking up the road that day, that none of us would ever reveal to anyone, not even our parents, where Salamander Pond was.

Lying in bed that night, trying to fall asleep, I was thinking about the vast treasure I just *knew* we were going to find Saturday in the shallow, sandy bed of Salamander Pond and the stream it fed. What, I wondered, would I do with all that treasure? New Beatles and Rolling Stones albums and lunchboxes, Vacu-Forms, and Schwinn banana-seated Sting-Ray bicycles galore for everybody I knew, I thought as I laid there, my eyes drifting out the window next to my bed and up into the stars. I could feel and smell the cool, early October night air gently blowing through the 3 inches of raised window as I stared at the stars and dreamed of my coming wealth, fame, and fortune.

And then, I remember being so scared so suddenly that I saw two of everything—as though I was cross-eyed from being hit in the forehead with a brick. Time stopped for a frozen instant. Nausea filled my stomach, and I immediately broke out in a cold sweat. The same whistling, the same strange, eerie melody my friends and I had heard in the woods earlier that day was coming through those 3 inches of open window next to my bed!

I was so frightened I couldn't move. Lying on my back, looking up at the ceiling in the dark, I could almost *feel* the whistling, it was so close. Close enough that I could hear whoever was whistling taking quick breaths in between the melody passages. I wanted to scream for my parents but was too scared to open my mouth. I tried to convince my arms and hands to grab the covers and pull them up over my head, but I was literally frozen in fear.

How had the whistler found me? We'd watched carefully behind us the whole way home from the woods and had seen nobody. It was only us four.

Ah hah! It suddenly hit me. It *had* to be one of my friends out there, standing in my driveway, whistling that stupid song in order to scare the bejesus out of me!

I unfroze from my fright, boiling into anger in the wink of an eye. I sat up, pushed the window screen all the way open, stuck my head out the window, and looked toward the end of the driveway, ready to yell and curse at whichever of my friends was trying to freak me out. There was nobody there.

Then, looking down, I saw him, standing in front of the garage and looking straight up at me—an old man, dressed all in black, like a preacher. Even his fedora was solid black. His white hair and side-burns stuck out slightly below the hat. As our eyes met, he began whistling that strange, scary tune.

I slammed the window down and dove into my pillow, covering my head and pulling all the covers over me in one quick motion. Shaking in fear, I prayed to God to protect me before, at last, mercifully, I cried myself to sleep.

The next morning at breakfast, I was afraid to tell my parents about the coin, the man in the woods who whistled at me and my friends and then chased us, or the visit he had paid me in the drive-way the night before. Besides, I'd promised my friends I'd never reveal the location of Salamander Pond, and if I *had* told my parents about the guy and the coin, I knew they'd have pried it out of me through the course of their ensuing investigation. I was trapped in secrecy and saw no way out.

What if this guy was some kind of maniac who was going to keep coming back until he killed me, my parents, and my sister and brother—maybe Donnie, Richard, and Bobby, and their families, too? How would anyone ever know what had really happened? Even at my young age, I remember thinking this was *way* too much for a 10-year-old. There had to be an answer before the guy either murdered us or drove me insane with fear by coming back and whistling that crazy song in the night.

My three friends and I met in the usual place that morning before our walk to school. It was way in the back corner of the field behind Donnie's house, on the edge of a huge apple orchard, and under a tall northern catalpa, or "Johnny Smoker" tree. We had a sort of a lean-to fort built back there where we'd meet and sometimes camp out overnight when it was warm out. It was our clubhouse, I guess you might say, but we just called it the fort.

As soon as my friends, who were all waiting for me, looked at me, and I looked at them, I stopped in my tracks and said, "What?" The three of them looked worried and scared.

"Did *you* hear anything last night?" Bobby said, in little more than a frightened whisper. They all looked at me intently.

"The whistle? The guy whistlin'? *You* guys heard it, too?" I demanded.

Sure enough, they'd all heard it, and it had scared them as much as it had me. None of them, however, had dared look out any windows to see *who* was doing the whistling. After talking about it for a few minutes, we figured out it was just about 10:30 when the whistler blew his serenade. Then I surprised the hell out of them.

"He was standing in my driveway, right in front of the garage. I saw him, man, and he saw me!"

My friends couldn't believe it as I told them how I'd seen the guy just standing there, looking up at me, whistling that tune. They were all visibly shaken by my story.

Then, incredibly, Bobby pulled out a piece of paper from his front pants pocket and unfolded it. Handing it to me, he said, "We found this tacked to the fort before you got here this morning."

There were three words on the white piece of paper: *PUT IT BACK*.

We all just stood there for a moment, the four of us, unable to comprehend the situation. Then, as if someone had switched on a light at the same instant in our fifth-grade heads, we said, "The coin! He wants the coin!"

I reached in my pocket and pulled it out, holding it for all to see in my open hand. It had all been about the coin. The whistling in the woods. The guy chasing us out of the woods. The eerie visit last night that we'd all heard, and now the note left tacked to the fort.

"But how the hell does this guy know where we live, and where the fort is?" Bobby demanded. "How does he even know we have the damn coin? Nobody else was around when you dug that up, Paul!" He paused, and then said, "So what do we do?" He looked like he was about to cry.

"We're putting it back!" I said. "What if he's a killer or a robber or something, and this is his?" I flipped the coin into the air and caught it. "That *has* to be what that note means. And it also means that he knows everything about us … where we live … where our fort is … our families—everything! I ain't messin' around with this no more! I'm takin' it back to Salamander Pond after school today. That's it!" There were no objections, but I was sure I heard some sighs of relief and saw three other heads bobbing up and down in agreement.

The longest, scariest walk I've *ever* had, through any woods, before or since, came that day after school as the four of us headed back to Salamander Pond. Every one of our senses was on high alert, finely sharpened and tuned. A twig breaking under our feet sounded like a .22 rifle being fired. Every movement, every sound caused us to pause and process it for a moment before continuing deeper into the woods.

After what seemed like an hour but was in reality only half that, we reached Salamander Pond. I pulled the coin from my pocket and, without hesitation, threw it into the spring. It hit the water before disappearing immediately under the soft sand, startling a salamander that darted for cover under one of the rocks on the side.

We looked at each other and listened, but all we heard was the soft gurgling of the spring and the calling of a few birds off in the distance. I was acutely aware of the smell of the forest and swamps in the area, and I was amazed that what had once been such a cool, beautiful place—a place that had given us so many hours of fun—had turned into a horror story for me and my friends.

"Let's get the hell out of here, now," I said. We left Salamander Pond that day never to return as a group again. That was October 1965.

About a year later, in early summer 1966, my parents bought a house in Collingswood, and we moved as soon as school ended. I would return now and again during that summer, taking the bus out of Collingswood to visit Bobby, Richard, and Donnie, but the visits became more and more infrequent, then stopped altogether as I began school in September at Zane North Elementary in Collingswood and made new friends.

One day, I was telling my new friends, Timmy, Jimmy, and Eddie, about the story of Salamander Pond, and all that had happened over the strange-looking, rock-encrusted gold coin I had found in it. Of course, they first became intrigued, but then Timmy, always skeptical by nature, said he thought the whole story was a load of BS. Jimmy and Eddie slowly started siding with Timmy's doubts, and before you knew it, they were calling me a liar and challenging me to break my oath of secrecy and take them to Salamander Pond.

What could I do? I was the new kid in town and didn't want to alienate my new friends. We planned a weekend trip to Salamander Pond.

The next Saturday morning the four of us got on the bus at the corner of Haddon and Collins avenues, having met around 8:30 AM at the corner store known as "The Triangle." I recounted the story in detail as we journeyed through South Jersey along Route 561 toward Salamander Pond.

I had taken my new friends along a different route through the woods because I didn't want to chance meeting my old friends, since I was breaking our sacred vow to never reveal the location of the spring to anyone. I knew these woods like the back of my hand, and I knew this new route would eventually bring us to Salamander Pond.

About 10 minutes into the woods, we saw a "Tarzan Swing"—a rope tied to a tree branch where you could swing out over the crick. I'd never seen this swing when I lived there, and I suggested we stop for a minute and try it out.

"Yeah, OK. You go first," said Jimmy, sitting down on a large tree root that was jutting out from the side of a hill. "I have to empty my sneaks of these damn pebbles, anyway."

I grabbed the rope and held onto it as I walked up the hill that I would launch myself from while sitting on the rope swing. As I was about to jump onto the rope, from somewhere in the woods, for all four of us to hear with our own ears, came the sound of someone whistling that haunting, evil-sounding tune I knew so well.

The four of us tore through those woods faster than lightning, running through swamps and sticker bushes and hitting our heads on low-hanging anythings and everythings. No one said a word until we were all seated in the rear of the bus, headed back toward Collingswood.

"I told ya's!" I said, smiling, looking across the seat at the three wide-eyed now-believers sitting next to me.

They never called me a BS-er again!

Over the years, I've written more than 1,000 songs in most every genre, being someone who enjoys all kinds of music, and I've made music one of my chosen professions in life. As a songwriter and composer, it's the norm that, at most times of the day or night, there's usually some sort of melody going on in my head. When I become aware of one, I try to write it down or record it somehow, so as not to forget it, and maybe employ it in a composition at some point. I have tried many, many times to recall and translate the whistled melody from the woods and the driveway that night onto paper or tape, but I simply cannot do it. I have come to believe that this tune wasn't meant to be recorded, only *heeded.*

Salamander Pond is still out there in the Pines, and, incredibly, it can be seen using Google Earth—*if* you know where to look. I believe the coin we found that day, and probably many others like it, remains there, buried in the mysterious sands of Salamander Pond.

Donnie, Bobby, and Richard long ago moved away from the town which I've gone out of my way not to reveal by name. Only the Good Lord knows how many performances from "the Whistler" I'd have to suffer through if I did. No, thank you. I don't ever want to hear that sound drifting on the night air again.

I think it's a safe bet that all four of us—actually, make that all *five*—will take the location of Salamander Pond to our graves!

Magic of the Silver Queen

For the longest time back in the late 1800s, folks in and around the Pine Barrens were fond of telling the tale about old JayBea's fruit and vegetable stand on Forked Neck Road in Shamong, and how, one summer, the first "Silver Queen" corn anyone had ever seen or tasted showed up there. That corn caused quite a commotion, because it put any and all other corn to shame with its sugarlike sweetness and tender eatin', and *that* is sayin' somethin', because everybody knows, and knew even back then, that Jersey corn is the best there is. But starting that summer, JayBea's was better than all the rest! And it all started with a chance meeting due to a case of the sniffles, an ancient Norse Rune necklace, and a plain, good old helping of gratitude and grace. And maybe some Pine Barrens magic thrown in by that kind old gypsy gal, Queeny, for good measure.

Jay (short for Jason) and Bea (short for Beatrice) Jennings were the hardest-working husband and wife farming team anyone ever had the pleasure of knowing. From well before sunup to long after sundown, they worked and worked and reworked that small farm of theirs that was nestled on the crook of the curve on Forked Neck Road. Tilling, planting, hoeing, weeding, and eventually harvesting their crops, they could be seen out there together, rain or shine, every day, coaxing some of the best tastin' fruits and vegetables imaginable out of that sandy Pine Barrens earth. The two were inseparable, and the folks who came from miles around by horse and buggy or on foot to buy their produce soon took to calling them simply "JayBea" (pronounced "JAY-bee"), no matter if one or both were standing there.

Once the crops started coming in around July-ish, Bea would assume the duties out at the wooden farmstand that Jay had built at the intersection of Forked Neck Road and Old Trenton Road, just up the way a piece from the farm. She never stood still, it seemed, while she sorted, stacked, wrapped, and otherwise arranged and rearranged and packaged the produce she sold at the stand. Folks in the area soon started referring to busy people as being "busy as Bea," which is how that phrase first came into use. Said correctly, it's actually "He's as busy as Bea," and why you'll often hear it nowadays as "busy as *a* Bea" is anyone's guess.

Every Friday, while Bea was tending to the chores at the stand, Jay would hitch up his team of two horses to a buckboard wagon, load it with bushels and boxes of fresh fruits and vegetables, dried corn, and oats, and haul them into Camden where he sold them to market owners. He'd leave very, very early in the morning and wouldn't return until very late at night, sometimes not 'til midnight. Jay enjoyed his trips into the city, save for the time he lost a wagon full of cracked corn that became uncovered and then rain-soaked while he was trying to help a crying old woman find a necklace she'd lost on the road.

Regardless of what time he returned home from his trip to Camden, Bea would be up waiting for Jay. She'd fix him a meal and have a hot bath ready for him, and she enjoyed hearing all the stories he would tell her about his trip and what he'd seen and done in the city, listening intently as she washed his back.

Queeny was a gypsy woman who lived out in the Pine Barrens, in a spot where, according to her, "the Old One says a kindly Mexican man will fall out of the sky someday." She would laugh and laugh, showing off the six teeth she had left in her mouth, as she added, "I might just catch him if I'm around long enough! Hah, hah!"

This old gypsy gal was well-known in Shamong for pitching crazy-sounding stories and predictions to those she met and talked to. Inevitably, during any conversation she ever had, her eyes would get wide, she'd look up, smile, and say something like, "the Old One says we're standing on top of an ocean that lots of folks are gonna come diggin' for soon," or "the Old One says somebody's gonna make candy out of that salty ocean water and become famous for it one day soon," or "the Old One says a great ball of fire is going to burst above these woods and somehow the whole world will hear it happen at the same time it's happening."

Queeny never told anyone who the Old One was, and most folks were afraid to come right out and ask, preferring to assume she meant the Christian God. By and large, people figured she had pulled up on the short straw whilst standing in the brain line and paid no mind to her predictions and stories anyway. She wore a silver talisman on a chain around her neck, and after each prediction, she would pull it to her lips and kiss it. It was shaped like a cock-eyed "L7" inside a circle. "It's a Rune called Jera," she would say to those who asked about it, "and it keeps the Old One whisperin' to me, *iffin* I kiss it after each time he's done a-whisperin'. It's *magic*!"

No one knew where Queeny was from or how long she'd been living deep in the Pine Barrens in that stick hut she called home. She had no family, no husband or children, but she seemed to be happy when anyone talked to her. She was always dressed in a long, black dress and a coat, when the weather called for it, and wore a purple babushka around her head that gathered her waist-long, silvery-white hair into a ponytail.

Every Friday at noon, Queeny would walk up to JayBea's stand, slap her hand on the counter board, and say, "Hey! Hey! JayBea Jay! Whatchya growed that's good today?" Queeny and Bea would laugh and laugh at the little rhyme each time Queeny recited it, which was every time she visited. They would chat for awhile about the weather or the events of the day, then Queeny would select the fruits and vegetables she wanted, and Bea would box them up or put them in a burlap sack.

Before leaving on one particular Friday, Queeny widened her eyes, looked up, and said to Bea, "The Old One says you got fields full o' sugar 'n gold comin', JayBea! Fields full o' sugar 'n gold! Hah, hah!"

Bea wrinkled her brow and said, "But, Queeny, we've no plans to grow sugarcane or anything of the like here. It won't grow in these parts, you know that."

Queeny smiled and said, "I'm just passin' on what the Old One says is all. Have a good six days 'til I see you in seven! Hah, hah!"

Then off she walked into the Pine Barrens with her bag of fruits and vegetables, kissing "Jera" as she whispered to herself.

It was to be the last time Bea would ever see the old woman.

During the next few days, Bea felt herself coming down with a cold. The runny nose, watery eyes, cough, and headache progressed, and she steadily felt worse and worse. By Thursday, she was completely exhausted, and that night, she told Jay she was afraid she wouldn't be able to manage her chores at the stand on Friday.

"No problem, Bea," Jay said lovingly to his sick wife. "What I have to take to the city can wait until you're feeling better. I'll tend to the stand tomorrow while you stay in bed and rest."

The next morning, Jay left his wife sleeping as he got up at the crack of dawn, fixed a breakfast of smoked ham and eggs for himself, and readied the stand for the day's business. At noon, he watched as an old woman came walking up to the stand, mumbling and smiling, showing off her six teeth. It was as though she was having a fine conversation with someone standing next to her, Jay thought. An invisible someone only she could see.

"Good day, ma'am," Jay greeted the old woman in a friendly voice. "What can I help you with today?"

Startled at hearing this man's voice and not Bea's, Queeny covered her mouth and chirped, "Oh!" Stopping cold in her tracks, she just stared at Jay for a few moments.

Finally, she moved her hand away from her mouth, and said, "It's *you*!"

"Yep, I'm me—at your service," Jay said with a chuckle, though feeling somewhat uncomfortable at this awkward meeting with the old woman.

"No, no. You don't understand. It's *you* … I finally found *you*!"

"Well, I've been here all along. Just on the farm, though, not here at the stand. The wife usually—"

"You're Bea's husband!" Queeny interrupted, more like a command than an inquiry. "And where is Bea?"

"The missus is in bed with the sniffles today," Jay said, rubbing his hands together and shifting back and forth on his feet, trying to conceal his discomfort. "And who might you be?"

"They call me Queeny," said the old woman.

"Of course!" Jay said. "The wife's spoken of you many times. I'm glad to finally meet you, ma'am."

Tears suddenly welled up in Queeny's eyes, and Jay took a step back in the stand, wondering what he had said to offend the old woman.

"But we *have* met before," she said in little more than a whisper. "On the road to Camden, long ago." Pulling her talisman out, she said, "You helped me find *this* and, in the process, you lost a wagonload of grain to that storm that came upon us. Remember?"

Jay looked closer at the talisman, then shifted his eyes and looked into Queeny's, and said slowly, "Well, I'll be damned … pardon me, I'll be *darned* … after all these years, here you are again!"

Queeny thought for a long moment before speaking. "For 27 years now, I've asked the Old One, every night, if he would bring us together once more so I could thank you specially before I go to my rest. I didn't think he was going to grant me that wish, but he has."

"No special thanks necessary, ma'am. It all worked out for the best," Jay said smiling, thinking to himself how much it had dented his income, throwing all that cracked corn away after he'd helped this woman find a necklace in the pouring-down rain and mud.

Queeny took something from her coat pocket and placed it on the counter. It was a scale model replica of a buckboard wagon that was the spitting image of Jay's. As she removed its cover, Jay saw it was a box, filled with dried corn kernels. She took off her talisman and chain, gently laid them on top of the corn, then put the cover back on the box and handed it to Jay. "The Old One will call me home on Tuesday morning, and I want you to have this," she said, looking him directly in the eye.

"Oh, no, ma'am. I can't take that from you," Jay said, trying to push the box back to Queeny. "Plus, the wife would never—"

"Shhhh!" Queeny said, holding a finger to her lips. "Let an old woman speak. You helped me find the most precious item I've ever owned when you didn't have to, when helping me was against your interest. You are kind at heart, with a good soul, and I want you to take this as a token of my thanks. *Please.* I was going to give it to Bea, thinking I'd never find you, but as it turns out you are husband and wife, and I couldn't be happier. Please take it!" She was nearly pleading.

Jay took the box into his hand, and said, stuttering, "Well … I guess … I mean, thank you *so* much, but you really don't have to—"

"Listen closely to what I say," Queeny interrupted him. "Leave the silver Rune and chain on top of the corn until it's time to plant next year. Do *not* separate the silver from those kernels. When planting time comes, be sure to plant each and every kernel, and keep them separate and away from any other seeds you plant. Do you understand?"

The old woman looked at Jay sternly as if to make her point, then smiled again. "Tell your wife I hope she gets well soon!" And, with that, she turned on her heels and walked off into the Pine Barrens with Jay calling, "Thanks, again!" over and over until she finally disappeared from sight.

That night, as Jay and Bea were having dinner, with Bea now feeling well enough to get up and around and cook a stew, he told her of the strange and fateful meeting with Queeny, and recalled what had happened on the road so long ago. He talked about the coincidence of Queeny having known Bea over the years, without realizing they were married until today, and about the buckboard box full of corn kernels, the necklace, and Queeny's strict instructions.

"She's going to be called 'home' on Tuesday by some old guy, I think she said, and that's why she brought it over to give to you."

"Did she say the Old One was calling her home?" Bea asked in a whisper.

"Yep, that's it!" Jay said. "It's the *Old One* who's going to be calling her." He laughed softy and shook his head. "I think she's nuts, Bea, to tell you the truth."

"She's often talked about the Old One at the stand," Bea said. "Of course, she says a lot of peculiar things and has some very interesting notions about the future. I certainly hope she's not sick or moving away." She put a hand on Jay's arm. "Did she really say the Old One was calling her home?"

"That's right," Jay said in between forkfuls of stew. "I put that box o' corn and the necklace she gave me in the drawer of the workbench out in the barn, by the way. I'll bring it in tomorrow. Right now I'm beat and need the bed!"

***

On the following Thursday, the news spread through the Pine Barrens as fast as word-of-mouth could spread that Queeny had been found dead and had *been* dead for 3 days. JayBea heard it first from Gary Kelley, a neighbor and steady customer. According to Gary, children playing in the woods had happened upon her body. She was to be cremated and her ashes sent to Norway, where, it turned out, she was born. Her real name was Ragnhild Thorbjornsen, and she was a high priestess in the Old Norse religion known as "Ásatrú."

"Turns out the old gal was a pagan, JayBea!" Gary said to the couple as they all leaned on the fence that surrounded the farm. "I always knew she was a little brain-touched, what with all that smilin' and whisperin' and predictin' those crazy happenings."

Bea thought for a moment and replied, "Yes, Gary, but it's not for us to hold another's religion in judgment. She was kind and decent, and a very good customer, too. She even gave us a gift last week, didn't she, Jay?"

"Yep, a box o' corn kernels and a silver necklace with a medal of some kind on it. I'm gonna plant the corn next year, is what she told me to do, and give the necklace to the missus. Who knows what'll grow up out there!"

"Might be a smart thing to throw that corn and necklace aside," Gary said, shaking his head. "The Lord only knows *what* could grow, comin' from an old gypsy-witch like that. And that necklace mighten choke the missus, hah, hah, hah! Gotta run now, JayBea—goo'bye."

Summer soon turned to autumn, and before anyone knew it, winter had set in on the Pine Barrens. The cold winds and heavy snows kept JayBea pretty much housebound, save for the "must-do" chores farming presents, which included chopping a *lot* of wood for fuel.

As March slowly melted into April, the soils in the Barrens defrosted, and finally, the new planting season was upon JayBea. As he readied his seeds and planting equipment, teaming up the horses and plow, Jay remembered Queeny's little buckboard box that he'd put in the drawer of his workbench. He took the box out of the drawer and carefully opened it. He saw the corn kernels, but the necklace and talisman were gone. Just then, Bea walked into the barn, bringing him a hot cup of coffee.

"Did you take the necklace from this box, honey?" he asked her.

"Why, no, of course not. I've never seen that box before." She paused and then said, "Is that the box Queeny gave you?"

"Yep, but the necklace and medal are gone, and it looks like the kernels have rotted or something. They're shaped funny and have a strange color. Best to chuck 'em in the pigpen, I guess."

"Jay, plant them," Bea said adamantly. "Plant them just like Queeny said to do—in her memory, and for me, OK?"

"OK, then, you're right," Jay said. "I'll put 'em in down on the lower acre. We'll see what happens."

Jay planted the kernels, and, as the corn grew, he watched its progress carefully, discovering something most unusual as the first ears started ripening: The kernels had a silvery-white look and were in perfect straight lines on the cob. When JayBea tried the first of the picked ears for dinner one night, they were astounded at the sweetness and tenderness of this unusual corn.

After dinner, JayBea stood on the porch and looked out over the farm.

"We have something quite special here, Bea darling," Jay said. "Something no one will ever believe, but tasting *is* believing, and that is the most delicious corn I've ever et. I am going to sell most of the crop, but I'm going to keep a goodly amount of seed to sell and so we can plant a larger crop next year. This is gonna change corn eatin' forever, Bea—and all thanks to that old gypsy woman!"

News got around the Pine Barrens quickly, and before long, it seemed *everyone* was coming to JayBea's stand on the Old Trenton Road, better known today as Route 206, to try this new, incredibly sweet and tender silvery-white corn. One July afternoon, neighbors Gary and Barbara Kelley came over to buy some.

"Was this corn growed from the seed that old witch left ya's with, JayBea?" Gary wanted to know.

"Sure was!" answered Jay.

"Didn't she leave a so-called magic necklace for you, Bea?" Gary asked. "I don't see it on ya."

Bea thought for a long moment before answering. She wanted to tell Gary it was rude of him to be prying into business that wasn't his, but she was quite fond of Barbara and wanted to keep peace with the neighbors.

"It's in the corn, Gary," she finally said, matter-of-factly. "The magic silver necklace, with the Jera—it's *in the corn*!"

They all laughed, except for Bea, who added, simply and slowly, "The magic is in the Silver Queen corn."

The name stuck, and it's been called that ever since. Today, anyone who has eaten it will tell you that there *is* magic in every mouthful of fresh, Jersey-grown Silver Queen corn. It is magically sweet and tender, whether steamed or roasted, slathered with butter and a pinch of salt and pepper, or eaten raw, right off the cob.

And to think it all began with a little wagon-box full of strange-looking kernels and a magic necklace given from one friend to another, in thanks for a good deed well done.

The Wind Song

The best drink of the night is the one *after* the gig is finished. Most of the crowd has gone (after telling you how much they enjoyed the show) and you're sitting there, feeling the warm glow that only "on" nights of playing for a live audience can give you.

Relaxing in the glow after another great night at the Green Bank Inn awhile back, I was approached by an old gentleman who had been enjoying the music all night. He walked right up to my table and sat down, like he knew me. I'd never seen him before in my life, yet he seemed so familiar.

But that's how it was in the Green Bank back when I played there regularly. Folks liked your music, and you wound up becoming fast friends pretty quickly and easily. Maybe it was the music and libations. Maybe it was the charm and mysteries of the inn itself, built in the 18th century as a stagecoach stop at the intersections of Routes 542 and 563, deep in the Burlington County Pine Barrens. Stories and rumors abound concerning Jersey Devil sightings, ghostly visitations, and other strange goings-ons in and around the place. I think the combination of all the above was what made a gig at the Green Bank so special.

"I'm Bull Parclasti," the old man said as he sat down. He sounded a little like he was from down south—but that's just what's known as the South Jersey drawl. "Down Jersey" sounds very "southern," especially from down around Millville and Vineland. And maybe, not coincidentally, that's because if the Mason-Dixon line had continued east across the Delaware River, it would have run right through the middle of South Jersey. It's also a known fact that many residents of "Deep South Jersey" sided with the Rebs in the Civil War. Anyway, ol' Bull Parclasti had a good bit of the "Jersey Drawl."

"Well, hell, Bull, I'm Paul. Set down a mint!" I extended my hand to him, and we both smiled, as he was already sitting.

"Lorraine, lemme get two shots of Dewars," I said to Lorraine, the owner and sometimes waitress (when "the Bank" is busy, or she just feels like it). She looked at me and raised one eyebrow.

"OK, then," she said, seemingly surprised.

When she returned with the drinks, she set them down, then bent over and kissed me. "Thanks, Paul. We drained the place tonight. You guys sounded great."

"My pleasure, doll," I said.

Bull picked up one of the shots, I picked up the other, and he said the toast, "To the Wind Song, Paulie-boy! May you hear it one day, and forget it the next!" We shot the Dewars.

"What the hell is the Wind Song, Bull?" I asked.

"Jesus, boy! You been playin' these woods for as long as I can remember, and *you* don't know what the *Wind Song* is?"

I smiled at Bull. I'd *never* seen him before, yet he seemed to know me and knew I'd been playing in the Pines for many years. But that's part of the charm of the folks who live here. They're very,

very clannish, and it's quite an honor for me whenever one of them thinks of me as one of their own.

"The Sammy Firesides thing, right?" I said.

"The same," he said. "Soooo, you've heard it then?"

Sitting there in the Green Bank Inn, which was built in the 1700s, the memory of the legend of the Wind Song came rushin' back to me.

Way back in the 1700s, before we were the United States, a fella by the name of Sammy Firesides frequented these parts, around what's now called Green Bank. Legend has it that right across the street from the Green Bank Inn, there was a little footbridge that crossed the Assunpink Crick. The story goes that Sammy, who was a young man at the time, would stand on that bridge till the wee hours of the morning, playing his fiddle along with the live music that came wafting out of the tavern, which, back in the day, was the *only* stagecoach stop between Tuckerton and Camden, and quite the popular hangout.

Apparently, Sammy's playing was so bad he was forbidden to bring his fiddle *inside* the Green Bank Inn.

One night, while Sammy was standing on the bridge playing, or trying to, the Devil came along, and said, "I will make you the best fiddle player in the world if you promise me you will write a melody, in my name, and that you'll play it whenever or wherever you play, at least once a night."

Sammy agreed.

The very next time musicians were playing in the Green Bank Inn, the musicians, as well as the patrons, heard beautiful fiddle music being played along with the band … but from outside. When they went looking for the source, there was Sammy playing his fiddle on the bridge.

The crowd invited Sammy into the inn, bought him drinks, and enjoyed his fiddle playing immensely. At the end of the night, just before the stage left for Camden, Sammy announced, "Listen, friends, to one more tune, if ya's will. It's a bit of a ditty o' mine, and it's called 'The Wind Song.'"

Sammy played the sweetest, yet most peculiar and eerie-sounding song anyone could remember hearing. Some folks started crying, the song evoked such emotion. Sammy finished the song and then left for parts unknown, into the wooded Jersey night, just before the stagecoach full of passengers left for Camden.

The next day, Green Bank, along with all the little towns along the Mullica River, buzzed with the news. The stagecoach that had left the Green Bank Inn the night before had gone off the bridge at Batsto into the river. There were no survivors.

It happened again, then again, and yet again. Seemingly every time Sammy would play his "Wind Song," a horrible fate would befall some or all of those who heard it. Rumor had it, around that part of southern Burlington County, that Sammy was in league with the very Devil himself, and "The Wind Song" was cursed.

Something had to be done.

The county's only sheriff, a man whose name has long since been forgotten, came up with a plan. A meeting with the men in town was called, and it was decided that he, the sheriff, would disguise himself as the stage driver, invite Sammy to go for a ride to Camden, and "dispose" of Sammy in the woods on the way.

The next night, Sammy took the bait. The sheriff and Sammy left the Green Bank Inn around 11 PM, and, sure enough, Sammy was playin' his "Wind Song" as they disappeared into the woods.

Neither man was seen or heard from again.

However, there are many, many folks who swear to this day that they hear, ever so faintly, the strains of a fiddle wafting through the cedar swamps in the Pine Barrens, late at night.

"Aw, hell, Bull," I laughed. "I might have heard it once or twice. When Lorraine was pourin' triples! Hah, Hah, Hah!"

Presently, Lorraine walked over to the table and said, "Paul, you OK?"

"Sure. In fact, let's have two more."

Again, she raised that eyebrow as she turned and went to get the drinks.

"A lot of folks dismiss that as hooey, Paulie-boy, but I'm here to tell you, there's more to it than what you might have heard. A lot of good pickers around here have met their deaths tryin' to figure out that goddamn song. It ain't nothin' to be pud-in' around with."

"I play what I write, Bull," I said. "I don't care about no 'Wind Song.' Don't worry about it."

"Well, boy, iffin' you hear it, you'll worry about it, all right. You'll have to, because it will eat you up. You hear me, Paulie-boy? It'll *eat you up*!"

Bull seemed genuinely angry all of a sudden. He got up and went to the men's room just as Lorraine came back with the next round.

"You sure you're OK? Your old lady OK?" she asked, affectionately referring to my wife, Cookie.

I was perplexed, since I was doin' what I always do. "Whatsamatta, doll?" I said. "You know I like to hang awhile after the gig."

"Well, you're really puttin' the shots down," she said, "and you're sittin' here talkin' to yourself, for Chrissakes. I thought somethin' might be wrong, is all."

"*Lorraine*! I'm sittin' here talkin' to that old man, Bull, and buyin' him a couple shots, is all. Christ!"

Up went the eyebrow. "What old man, Paul?"

"The guy who just went into the men's room. He's been sittin' here talkin' to me for at least half an hour!"

Lorraine actually walked into the men's room. Then I heard her yell, in Lorraine fashion, "There ain't a swingin' dick in here, Paul!"

She came out and walked back to my table. "I'm callin' your old lady."

***

That was nearly 10 years ago. Today, I took my grandson into the Pine Barrens for a hike in the woods. About five miles west of the Green Bank Inn, in a little town called Pleasant Mills, we came upon a long-forgotten, grown-over cemetery. I lifted one of the old tablet-style headstones that had fallen over, and we brushed it off, hoping to read what had been etched into it.

I could barely breathe as my eyes took in the words. My grandson, staring at me with wide eyes, said, "Pop! Why are you shakin'?"

I read the inscription aloud:

BULL PARCLASTI
Born 1702 Died 1758
Here lies our Sheriff
Who toiled long.
No more Wind.
No more Song.

Goodbye, for Now

Well, then … We've shared some songs and some stories about my Pine Barrens, haven't we?

I sincerely hope you enjoyed hearing them as much as I enjoyed bringing them to you.

And who is to say which ones are fact and which ones are fancy?

Be that as it may, I think you now understand why my Pine Barrens are so very special—if you didn't already.

I'd sure like to see you here for a visit sometime, so that you can enjoy all the special things the Pine Barrens has to offer. But please, if and when you do come, be very careful about fire, and make sure you leave the Barrens in the same beautiful way that you found them.

I hope we'll meet again, here on my porch, in the light of the moon, and share some more stories and songs real soon.

Stories from the south of Jersey.

Stories from the Pine Barrens.

About the Author

Born and raised in southern New Jersey, Paul Evans Pedersen Jr. fell in love with the Pine Barrens in 1962, on his first camping trip with Haddonfield's Boy Scout Troop 64. In the dead of night, the campsite was visited by what Paul and his fellow campers—and, indeed, the troop leader himself—believe was the Jersey Devil. Having survived the incident, Paul found himself captive to the many lures and charms of the Pine Barrens, and inspired by its stories and songs to become a writer.

An avid collector of antique glass bottles, Paul has traveled throughout the Pine Barrens in search of these and other treasures—as well as spent time entertaining in Pinelands bars and taverns—fueled his curiosity about South Jersey's "primeval backyard" and the people and creatures who call it home. Many a story flowed from Paul's pen after a day or night spent exploring the swamps, sugar-sand roads, and out-of-the-way watering holes of the Pine Barrens.

In addition to writing short stories, Paul is an accomplished songwriter, performer, screenwriter, journalist, and photographer. He has been a reporter for *The Hammonton Gazette*, *Hammonton News*,

Daily Journal (Vineland), and *Retrospect Weekly*. He has worked as a professional firefighter in both New Jersey and Houston, Texas, and as a volunteer firefighter in Collingswood, New Jersey.

A prolific songwriter, Paul's songs have been widely recorded and can be heard on both terrestrial and satellite radio locally, nationally, and internationally. Among his notable hits are "Cape Lonely," performed by Michael Mason, and "The Screamin' Hollar Inn," performed by Paul, as Paul Evans, on the album *Agua Noir*. Seven of Paul's songs, all sung by his wife, Cookie, appeared on the soundtrack of the 2012 movie *Breathless*, starring Val Kilmer, Gina Gershon, and Ray Liotta.

As a performer, Paul has been singing and playing drums and guitar in bands from the time he was 12. In the 1990s, he toured the U.S. and Canada with the Hall Of Fame Show out of Nashville, Tennessee, which featured such country music greats as Bill Monroe, Grandpa Jones, Hank Thompson, Johnny Paycheck, Little Jimmy Dickens, and Jeannie C. Riley. A South Jersey favorite, Paul performs locally whenever he can.

In 2009, Paul self-published *Required Restroom Readings*, a collection of his short stories and Haiku poetry. He has developed many of his short stories into screenplays.

Paul is known to South Jersey fashionistas as the inventor and maker of "Pine Barrens Diamonds," a line of jewelry he handcrafts from antique glass. He lives in Elm, New Jersey, with Cookie, with whom he shares four children, 10 grandchildren, and one overgrown blond Labrador retriever.

He is currently working on his first novel.

Also From Plexus

Pioneer, Go Home!

A novel by Richard Powell

The novel that might have been called *Piney, Go Home!* delivers a fast-paced story, a terrific cast of characters, and dozens of memorable, laugh-out-loud moments. This 50th anniversary edition restores Richard Powell's *New York Times* bestseller and includes a previously unpublished preface by the author. *Pioneer, Go Home!* relates the adventures of the Kwimpers—a motley clan of New Jersey Pineys who break down on the side of a southern highway project and decide to claim squatter's rights. Hilarity ensues as the family defends its homestead against an onslaught of conniving bureaucrats, Mother Nature, and the mob.

280 pp/softbound/ISBN 978-0-937548-71-4/$15.95
Ebook also available

Voices in the Pines

True Stories from the New Jersey Pine Barrens

By Karen F. Riley; Foreword by John Pearce

From true life tales of murder and mayhem to inspiring accounts of triumph over adversity and "Pineys" fighting to protect their way of life, *Voices in the Pines* brings the storytelling legacy of the Pine Barrens into the 21st century. Author Karen F. Riley—a South Jersey transplant by way of Brooklyn, New York—roamed the woods, rural communities, and farms of the Pinelands in search of compelling stories. The result is an engrossing human journey into the heart of the Pines. You'll meet artisans, activists, farmers, educators, local heroes, and regular folks in this collection of true stories—told in the words of those who lived them.

232 pp/softbound/ISBN 978-0-937548-67-7/$15.95
Ebook also available

A Field Guide to the Pine Barrens of New Jersey

Its Flora, Fauna, Ecology and Historic Sites

By Howard Boyd

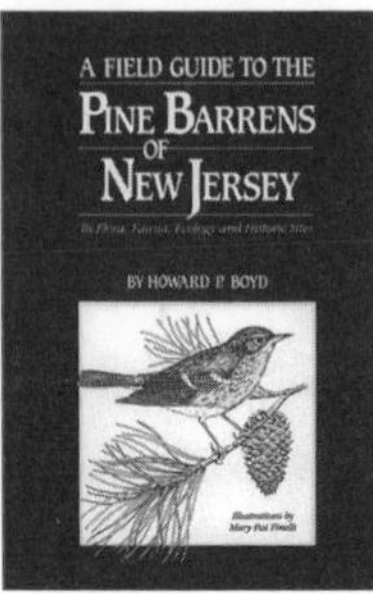

Howard P. Boyd presents readers with the ultimate handbook to the New Jersey Pine Barrens. Boyd begins his book by explaining and defining what makes this sandy-soiled, wooded habitat so diverse and unusual. Each entry gives a detailed, non-technical description (for more than 700 species) of a Pine Barrens plant or animal, indicating when and where it is most likely to appear. Complementing most listings is an original ink drawing that will greatly aid the reader in the field as they search for and try to identify specific flora and fauna.

436 pp/softbound/ISBN 978-0-937548-19-6/$22.95
436 pp/hardbound/ISBN 978-0-937548-18-9/$32.95
Ebook also available

People of the Pines

By Bob Birdsall

Bob Birdsall celebrates the people and traditions of the Pine Barrens of New Jersey in this beautifully illustrated volume. Birdsall's perceptive lens and engaging text illumine more than two dozen individuals and their ways of life—many of which are fast vanishing. From "Piney" hunter-gatherers who still live off the land to hardworking baymen and farmers to volunteers and public servants, artisans and entrepreneurs, scientists, conservationists, and educators, these men and women typify the bold and creative spirit of the region.

160 pp/hardbound/ISBN 978-0-937548-63-9/$39.95

To order or for a catalog: 609-654-6500, Fax Order Service: 609-654-4309

www.plexuspublishing.com